# The Groundskeeper

## And Other Short Stories

## by Matt Shea

"The Groundskeeper And Other Short Stories" by Matt Shea. ISBN 978-1-60264-625-4.

Published 2011 by Virtualbookworm.com Publishing Inc., P.O. Box 9949, College Station, TX 77842, US. ©2011, Matt Shea. All rights reserved. No part of this publication may be reproduced, stored in a retrieval system, or transmitted in any form or by any means, electronic, mechanical, recording or otherwise, without the prior written permission of Matt Shea.

Manufactured in the United States of America.

# Dedication

These writings are dedicated to Frank and Vyerl Shea: alias mom and dad. They gave us that happy household on Ferdinand Street that had an open door policy for the entire neighborhood. It was their rule to always have enough food for everyone. Thanks for the great childhood!

Love,
    Mathew Joseph

# My Inspiration

My daughter, Laura is my only child. We have been through it all throughout her childhood. She rarely asked for anything. Instead, she would show me what she accomplished- and share it. When I retired in 2010, she bought a laptop and demanded that I pursue my dream of writing. When I would read her my early manuscripts, she would listen with pride and encouraged me. She gave me that push I needed to get started.

We made it, Laura!

Thanks,
Dad

# Special Thanks

Renée Klause is a special friend that was with this project from stem to stern. She reviewed these stories and gave advice that helped shape things for the better. She also took my portraits and even shared her fantastic Golden Retriever, "Dolly".

Thanks, Renée!
Matt

# Contents

# Tales from the Factory

Tales from the Hood...?

# THE GROUNDSKEEPER

IT WAS ANOTHER GLORIOUS Monday morning. The Freewater Ecology plant was vacant from the weekend but alive with spirit. Beautifully landscaped shrubbery outlined peaceful green grass covered by morning dew. All was now being awakened by the spectacle of sunrise. The rich golden brown soil under the tall trees was exposed by the advancing rays. The parking lot was clean, bare, and quiet. All was not as good as it seemed though. This serenity was on the verge of extinction, unless a miracle could happen.

A lone car cautiously entered the lot, almost an hour before start time. This was Jeremy Coat's first day as a bonded contractor. The zealous tradesman arrived early to assure a perfect attendance underway. He was in awe of the tranquility that greeted him. This wonderment of God's nature was enhanced by the sounds of undisturbed wildlife. The peaceful setting before human intervention made time stand still. Every precious second of this well preserved haven was being savored. Suddenly, there was a startling tapping on the window. He was relieved to find a seemingly harmless old man. The tall, lanky posture with a friendly smile and soiled coveralls put Jeremy at ease. Upon opening the window, the stranger spoke.

"I bet you're that contractor we're expecting! My name is Carl Goodwin, and I've been the groundskeeper here for the past forty years. I was told we hired an ambitious young man to help us out. Since I'm always the first one here every morning, I thought I'd drop by to say hello and welcome you aboard!"

"Well thank you," exclaimed a polite youth. "My name is Jeremy Coats; did you create all this beauty I'm looking at?"

"No," said the warm senior; I only do my part to respect it. Someone else gets credit for creating it!" The driver could only smile in agreement with the God-fearing man. Then Carl extended his hand to shake Jeremy's and continued. "It's getting close to start time; soon, many cars will be here and then it will get noisy. I always felt that this was  the best part of the day."

"I have to agree with you," responded the nineteen year old.

It was now twenty minutes before starting time. One by one, the vehicles showed up. In no time at all, the lot was full. "I better get in; I have to report to my supervisor," stated the enterprising youth. "I'm glad to have met you, Carl!"

The humble soul replied, "The feelings the same and have a good day!"

Jeremy knew where to go. He'd already met with the Plant Manager, John Bishop. The previous week, the two had agreed on a contracting bid that he submitted. The rest of the day would be spent moving tools and placing a metal garbage container outside for his projects.

The following morning, Jeremy arrived to  work in the same fashion. The parking lot was desolate and peaceful. The sun was just casting its eloquent light on the paradise he'd discovered the day before. He couldn't believe that this Eden was always there.

A movement at the far end of the lot distracted his thoughts. He was relieved to see the smiling face of his new friend. The caring elder must have anticipated another visit. As he approached, steam could be seen rising from two cups of coffee. The prompt workingman got out of his car to meet the congenial old-timer. "Good morning, Carl," greeted Jeremy.

"Good morning," replied the contented man, "you seem to be earlier this time. Let's have some coffee; follow me!" Jeremy wasn't familiar with the grounds. He was led down a beautiful path to a quaint bench. The setting was private and secluded from the trail that led them there. It was cloaked by the surroundings of beautiful bushes and ferns.

"Hey, that's quite a mug you have there," exclaimed the jubilant teenager as he pointed to  Carl's cup.

"Why, thank you; my granddaughter made this for me. It was a Father's Day gift, since she calls me dad. That child never knew her real father." Then in victory, he held up the heirloom and chuckled, "Isn't it great!" The happy grandfather then changed subjects. It became apparent that he wanted to discuss an important issue with the new employee. "Do you know why you were awarded this contract?"

"Because I was willing to give the lowest bid," answered the young business man.

The patriarch looked directly at Jeremy with his steel blue eyes and said, "There is more to it than that."

"What do you mean?" asked the puzzled youth.

Carl then asked, "Why did you decide to be a contractor?"

"I wanted to be like my uncle," replied Jeremy. "He seems to have everything: a big house, two cars, a truck, boat and trailer. He makes a lot of money. Sometimes, he gets paid for not doing much. He knows how to bid on a job and always makes it look good when it's finished. I was taught how to make a good living with this trade."

A disappointed Carl looked down as he absorbed the answer from the young apprentice. He then injected his years of wisdom. "You need to look beyond money; sometimes it's all about contributing. This is a community that's struggling with hard times. Money is not all there is to life. We're all sacrificing. You were chosen because we could see your good character. You can help us "turn the tide;" life will reward you later."

6

Jeremy sat still for several minutes and remarked, "This is not my home; I am just a contractor."

The wise man asked, "What did John Bishop actually tell you to do?"

The fledgling concentrated on the question and answered, "Nothing; all he did was show me the many things that needed attention. I appreciated that; it's my decision what I will tackle."

Carl then pointed out, "Did you notice that he didn't mention how far you can go? He didn't even say how long you could take. He gave all of us the same option. The state might shut us down if things don't pick up. We are doing everything we can to think of to attract more contracts."

It was now close to seven o'clock, and Jeremy had to start work. "Thanks for the coffee," said a confused youth.

"You're always welcome and have a great day," replied the father figure.

Several days later, the morning was engulfed with rain as Jeremy arrived to work. Like "Old Faithful," his buddy was there once again to share coffee. Carl yelled out to Jeremy, "Get your coat on and follow me!"

With enthusiasm, Jeremy donned his jacket and followed the frisky old man. This time he was led down a different trail. Together, they ran through the drenching rain and soon took shelter in a gazebo. Like all of Carl's world, this was accompanied by beautiful plants and hanging flowers. The fragrance of fresh blossoms seemed to be a trademark for this happy man.

"Wow," exclaimed Jeremy, "you cover all the bases!"

"I try," laughed the gentleman. The violent rain made a methodical sound as another morning was being shared. It seemed that these were the moments when the junior wanted to learn more about Carl.

"I have been meaning to ask you something," stated the pupil.

"Shoot," responded the professor.

"You mentioned cutbacks. Are you a victim of that?" asked Jeremy.

"We all are," answered Carl.

Jeremy reluctantly asked, "How many hours do you get to work a week?"

He looked at Jeremy and said, "As many as I want to."

The sapling continued to question, "How many hours do you get paid for?"

Carl Goodwin looked off in the distance responding, "It works out to be about thirty hours a week."

Like an inquisitive child, the young man asked, "Why do you do it?"

A long pause built up to his answer. With dignity, the proud man exclaimed, "Because I'm here!"

The novice contractor allowed that message to digest. After a few minutes passed, he was finished with his coffee. "I have to go now," said Jeremy.

"You have a good day," responded Carl.

Jeremy was consumed by the morning conversation. He realized he could still accomplish plenty with minimal expense - and still earn a fair income. His priority was directed to repairing easy projects: Leaking faucets, rewiring broken lights, and caulking windows.

Days later, the clear skies along with a wet environment made the grounds inviting for Jeremy. Again, there was the old man with the traditional coffee. Jeremy was like a puppy discovering his master's return.

"You've been the talk of the plant; everyone has noticed how hard you've been working," Exclaimed Carl as he handed him a hot cup of coffee.

"I'm glad you understand why I haven't been here; I've been starting earlier! I didn't want you to think that I had abandoned you," replied the reunited friend. Jeremy gazed at the good man and said, "I really look forward to seeing you."

The caring soul responded, "Hey that's my line!"

The youth continued with more questions. "Tell me Carl, why have you stayed here all these years?"

With pride, he looked toward the sky and replied, "My late mother was an original employee here seventy years ago. She was this building's first receptionist. In those days, this was a county building where families came for help. Eventually, it became the ecology department, with many additions added on. The current main entrance is part of that construction. If you inspect the "back" of this structure, the original entryway is still there. It was the best feature this campus had.

That main lobby has tall, majestic brass doors that led to a cobblestone road and gave access to where my mother worked. There is a fountain in the center where cars could drive around. It has benches surrounded by lovely wrought iron street lamps. Baskets were suspended from those polls, and they always had beautiful flowers in them. It was the best place in the county where we could play with other children.

Today, that lobby has been forgotten. The brass doors only serve as a barrier that hide the disgrace of what neglect has done. The years of growth prevents the doors from opening. What they would expose looks like an unclaimed dump. I do my best not to let that happen on this side."

Carl couldn't bear the thought of this tragedy. The depressed gray haired man walked away with his head hung low. Jeremy Coats had a different reaction; he now had a cause!

The aggressive laborer started his shift walking behind the plant to see its original entry. The old growth didn't allow him to get close. He could only view it from the trail leading to the gazebo. What he saw from the vantage point was thick brush that showed no signs of civilization. It appeared as undeveloped acreage that could serve as a refuge for wildlife. Going back through the new entrance, he eventually found his way to the old lobby.

The mammoth brass doors were testimony of the glory days. They were strong and mighty. It seemed like the dull sturdy barriers only needed to be freed from its unkempt environment. The lobby, however, was a disgrace. It had been abused as a makeshift storeroom for various items. Dried out buckets of paint, boxes of outdated county records, and rejected old furniture dominated the once proud room. This dumping ground buried the soul of the building and endless dust confirmed forgotten history. However, the room itself wasn't damaged.

The first task would be to remove the waste. The conscientious apprentice inspected every item before discard. Then, there came a discovery: a buried cardboard box in the corner of the room. Upon opening came the final inspiration needed to fuel his conquest. It contained the original wall hangings, plaques, and newspaper articles that inaugurated the opening of the grand building. Jeremy sat down and carefully examined the boxed contents. Everything was professionally framed and at one time displayed in the lobby.

Then he found the "Holy Grail!" Pictures of the original employees accompanied with the mayor and governor were found. The eight member staff was identified by name. The only female in the picture was a smiling woman by the name of "Clair Goodwin."

"This room will be restored to its original state," vowed a dedicated Jeremy Coats. The memorabilia would once again be hung on the walls of the old county building. They would be enshrined in the very room where that receptionist lived out her career!

The antique setting still held its charm: Beautiful oak window frames matched the molding on the ceiling and floors. The marble floor tiles only needed cleaning, not replacing. Sturdy Roman pillars supporting the ceilings only needed a fresh paint job and good lighting. This grand lobby of last century could be restored at a minimal cost.

The determined contractor then took his crow bar in an attempt to pry one of the doors open. Systematically, he kept relocating the leverage bar until he established a secure hold. With all of his might, he tried to open it. There was a loud groan from the frozen hinges as they resisted movement. He continued the effort by applying all his weight on the bar. The stubborn door budged two inches, with the movement disturbing many years of growth. The top of the door separated itself from old bird nests, decayed vines, and the buildup of dirt. This compost fell on the floor, engulfing the room with a cloud of dust. There was much work for one man, but the hours involved wouldn't matter.

The following day manifested the ritual between the two friends as they shared coffee in the picturesque setting. Jeremy was quiet on this morning. He was secure, now that he had direction. Carl asked him what was on his schedule that day. The reserved talent didn't tell him what he was actually doing and only acknowledged that he was swamped with work. They wished each other a good day and parted.

Carl noticed as Jeremy returned to his car and began to remove items. He was surprised to see that Jeremy had actually brought supplies from home. Upon seeing Carl, he stated, "It only takes up space at home, and I have a use for it here." He looked at the master and stated, "I like how you think."

"I like how you are thinking," responded Carl. The friends then wished each other a good day, shaking hands as they parted.

Plant wide, everyone noticed the intense work the new contractor was giving. Rumors traveled that he was actually renovating the old lobby. It was obvious to all that he was inspired by the most respected man in the county: Carl Goodwin. Like Carl, the handyman adopted  the culture of working resourcefully, with profit not being an issue.

The next sunrise, Jeremy made his way to the familiar bench and sat next to his confidant. Coffee was shared as the beauty of Carl's world controlled the moment. The male bonding continued as he began to ask more questions. "Do others share this place as you and I do?"

"Yes," stated the compassionate man. "Everyone here seems to find their time for this seclusion. The break time here varies from each department and  so does the lunch hour. Some stay here awhile after work; I even have those who visit here during the weekend. What I notice is the respect; nobody here would dare think of littering. If any litter is spotted, it's immediately picked up. There is no yelling around here either. Through time, this became a sanctuary for all of us."

Jeremy could only sit back and marvel at  what the reverent man had created for everyone. "I want to start early today," said a motivated worker.

"I have done that many times myself," replied Carl. "Let's have another good day!" Jeremy nodded with a smile. The comrades shook hands and embarked for their chores.

Jeremy was still working on the old lobby. The materials he had brought from home were enough to accomplish this task. The metal dumpster was almost full from the remnants that had collected through the years. Fresh paint had been applied to the walls and pillars. The wood was treated with polish and the windows were clean. The marble floors and main doors were buffed to their original color. Most importantly, the framed documented history was cleaned and displayed once again.

The old lobby was now looking like its first day in existence. It was clean, dusted, and regained its shine. The brass doors were the "Mount Everest" of the project; Jeremy knew that they functioned and didn't need replacing. It was just a matter of prying them open and facing the jungle that waited. He approached the metal barriers with determination. If he could open the first door completely, then the second would easily follow. With all of his strength committed to the task, he manipulated the door with the leverage bar. The groan from aging hinges battled the effort, but the tenacious contractor would not surrender. Eventually, the door gave way. There was something different this time; there was no fog of falling debris. Instead, brilliant rays of sunlight outlined the door. As he pushed, the Gothic metal wall opened, and Jeremy was stunned!

The cobblestone road was exposed! All of the tall grass, weeds, and blackberry bushes were removed. The famous fountain was no longer hidden in shame. Wrought iron flower baskets hung from the lamp posts. He was entering a world of yesterday!

Seated on a metal bench was Carl, holding two glasses.

"Do you think you can get this fountain running?" asked the groundskeeper.

With conviction, the contractor exclaimed, "I'll have it running in one day!"

"Well good," remarked the senior. "That would give me time to place the flowers I ordered in those baskets. It looks like you could use a break, care to join me?"

"I'd love to," answered a fatigued worker. He sat down with Carl as a cold drink was being handed to him. With mutual respect, they toasted one another on a job well done!

The aging soul spread out his arms, as if to hug the resurrected structure. "Do you see this?" asked the trembling old man. "It's what I had as a child!" A long moment passed as memories danced in his head. He then looked at his accomplice and asked, "Why did you do all of this?"

The young man looked at his mentor and proclaimed, "Because I'm here!"

Carl Goodwin could only smile at the prodigy in admiration. "I have some good news," he exclaimed. "The City Council dropped by today and liked what they saw. They have chosen this site for a Town Meeting. It's in recognition of the oldest county building being restored. They will be awarding state contracts and told us that we're first in line!"

Lemonade was the perfect drink for this hot afternoon. The men leaned back in admiration as a seventy year old life was being awakened. The landmark seemed to glisten in response as the air filled with an aura of gratitude and appreciation. A loving feeling could be felt drifting through the open door, as if to identify a child that used to play here.

# THE TRUTH CHAMBER

THE VIOLENT TREMOR shook the hallway as office doors opened. All personnel ran into the lobby to find where the disturbance was coming from. An apologetic management team could be seen in front of the conference room with Matt Berkley. Systematically, they were trying to calm down the disgruntle employee.

In recent years, the relationship between Matt and his boss had deteriorated. The tension between the two was so great that the entire plant could feel it. A much needed meeting was underway to address this issue. Whether the damage was beyond repair or the wrong thing was said, the situation only worsened. Matt even stormed out of the room, slamming the door with all his might. The scene was a page out of professional wrestling as the big mountain man drew attention with his theatrical display.

Meanwhile, Matt's boss, Jim Fairchild, looked on in bewilderment. The tall, clean-cut, athletic deacon was in shock over the accusations he just received. With dignity, he remained composed- nodding his head in disbelief. He was then escorted away from the melee by the plant manager and led to his office. Upon entering the room, the door was immediately closed.

Matt was more fortunate. He attended this meeting during his vacation, allowing him to leave without saying a word. The frustrated titan left the building with an abandoned feeling of hope.

Approaching his car, a familiar figure stood next to it. This was Archie White, Matt's closest friend on the job.

"Hey, I thought you were off this week," said the husky country boy as he spit tobacco on the dirty pavement.

"I am, but I had to attend a meeting with my boss this morning," said Matt.

"How are you two getting along anyway?" asked Archie.

"Bad," stated the gentle giant. "Either one, or both of us won't be working here soon."

"How can you be so sure of that?" asked the wise "Okie."

"We keep having our friction. This morning's meeting became a yelling contest...I wonder if I still have a job down here," retorted Matt.

"I have an idea; we're overdue to have a beer together! Would you like to meet after work?" suggested Archie as he punched his friend in the arm.

18

Matt answered with a chuckle, "That sounds great!"

"Well good! There is a little tavern by my place. How about meeting me there at seven o'clock tonight? I can tell that you need to get something off your chest," stated the concerned fishing buddy.

"Boy, you can say that again," laughed Matt. "I'll see you at seven tonight."

Archie then gave Matt his traditional "thumbs up." Matt acknowledged him with a smile and left the plant.

It was ten minutes to the hour when Matt entered the bar. Archie was already there and had two beers opened at a corner table. The stage was well set for listening to a troubled friend. Matt sat down, and Archie handed him a bottle. Archie then tapped his bottle with Matt's to confirm the long friendship.

"Matt, I love you," expressed Archie. "Everyone hates seeing you and Jim having battles. You're both great guys. What's wrong?"

The big man hung his head to focus on his thought. He then looked at Archie directly in the eyes and said, "He keeps changing my job; it's not the good old days anymore."

"Those days are gone, but the friendships haven't changed a bit," explained Archie. "You and Jim are actually old friends, just like us." Archie leaned back to allow his comment to digest as more silence passed.

"I don't believe that he's following orders from above," Matt replied.

19

The weathered face stared directly at Matt and said, "I can prove that he is."

Matt was mystified as he looked at his big brother figure. "If you can do that, it would solve everything! I would then know he wasn't out to get me and that I was only being paranoid," replied Matt. "I miss my old friend Jim Fairchild!"

Archie's love for his fellow man was directed at Matt. His radiant smile of truth did not require any words.

Matt could only raise his beer and cheer his friend. He then leaned forward, and in a quiet tone asked, "Now tell me, how you can prove this?"

The rugged farm boy looked up with a fearful expression and said, "I hope that I'm not making a mistake sharing this with you. Do you know my job very well?"

"Not really," said Matt with curiosity. "You cover the entire plant and basically all shifts! You are the "jack of all trades" that everyone leans on...a lot!"

Archie trembled as he looked at the innocence of his colleague. With a tear running down one eye, he said, "I would never wish this on anyone, but I think this would give you the answers you need."

"Tell me, Archie," replied a reluctant Matt.

"I have never shared this with anyone," said the leery confidant. "Can I trust you with this secret?"

"I promise," answered Matt.

"There is an old part of the plant that was a boiler room. When I started here thirty years ago, the boilers were being replaced with the generators we now have. Since then, office space was built on top of the original structure. Some of the pipes were never removed, just left in the old concrete. They lead up to the ventilation system in the northern part of the new offices. Whenever there is a meeting in Jim's office, I can hear everything through the old pipes," confided Archie.

"Where are they?" grinned Matt.

"That old shed where I keep my tools was the tool shed for the boiler room," explained Archie. "If you open it up, you'll see the back side of the shed blocked by the water main. If you get on your hands and knees, you can squeeze between the water main and the wall closest to it. There's actually an opening that allows you to get to the other side of the wall. That's where the old pipes are exposed. I drape a pair of coveralls from the hook above it to make sure nobody can see the hole. The coveralls are an old pair that nobody would ever think of taking. Once you get inside, it's dark and has a chair that someone must have put there long ago.

Since you're off this week, your car won't be in the parking lot. There is a meeting in Jim's office tomorrow; I think it's a top secret. They're to meet at seven p.m. after everyone has gone home."

"Can you get me in there tomorrow?" asked an excited Matt.

"Sure I can," replied Archie. "That's the easy part. Do you think you can actually sit down and hear

21

everything? You will hear some juicy stuff about everyone, including yourself! Remember, if you can hear them, they can hear you. To get caught, we would probably both get fired! Can you accept listening to a room full of people talk about you, with the belief that you aren't present? You can't bring a light- they might notice it whenever those pipes are exposed to sound. However, you will learn some secrets about this place and realize that your boss doesn't always have it so good.

You will never be able to look at them the way you do now, not after what you'll hear. It's a "truth chamber;" you will never be able to erase what this actually does to you." Then Archie White looked at his friend and asked, "What's your decision?"

Matt was speechless with the realization of this "Pandora's box." After a long moment of silence, the challenged man calmly said, "I have to. I need to know the truth about Jim and myself."

"Okay," remarked Archie with caution. "Tomorrow after work, I will leave at my normal time and go straight to your place. We'll return to the plant around five p.m.; I guess I'll be sneaking you in. If we're confronted by anyone, you'll be hiding in the back of my truck. I'll make it look like I forgot to lock my tool shed. You have a cell phone, and I'll drive by on the hour. When the office lights are out and the parking lot is empty, I'll call you. Remember, stay put and be quiet at all times. Wait for me to contact you. Agreed?"

"Agreed," answered Matt.

It was now past four o'clock the following afternoon. A pizza and salad awaited on the host's dining room table. The distinct knock on the door could only be Archie as Matt eagerly answered it. His guest was greeted by the aroma of good food and a handshake. The two bachelors relaxed and enjoyed dinner. Their conversation didn't reflect on the evening before. They simply looked at each other and reminisced on the many good times they had shared. Once dinner was finished, Archie said, "Let's go."

They arrived at the plant with no one present. Archie opened his unlocked tool shed and removed the dirty coveralls draped over the obscure entrance. He quickly got on his hands and knees and slithered into the abandoned chamber. He then turned on a flashlight and motioned for Matt to join him.

"Stay low; we don't have much room here," instructed Archie. The two were now sitting on the original concrete floor of the plant. Archie shined the light to show the dangerously low ceiling. He then exposed the vintage office chair in the corner. Earlier that day, Archie had draped a clean blanket over the chair with a second blanket neatly folded for warmth. "Get in the chair," whispered the commander. Matt sat in the chair, and then Archie covered him with a blanket exposing only his head. "Are you comfortable," he asked. The soldier nodded his head up and down to acknowledge their vow of silence.

"Here's what I'm talking about," continued Archie. He illuminated the top part of the wall facing the chair. There they were: three suspended metal pipes. They were crudely cut from their origins and were now a permanent fixture in the new plant. The exposed rusted flues could remind one of the eerie sensation when a tragic shipwreck was discovered.

The Gothic funnels had sharp - uneven openings that strangely pointed to the chair. The setting was that of a medieval torture chamber. The small confines made it impossible to stand. The dark space smelled of decay with dust, dirt, and oil. The walls echoed noises from the abandoned concrete. The jagged edges from the primitive chutes could easily cut human skin and the discolored iron would ensure infection. If Matt was to lean back and look up, the pipes would face him: point-blank.

"You don't have to go through with this," cautioned Archie.

A courageous Matt responded, "I have to; maybe I deserve this."

"I'll call you when they're all gone," said the guide as he patted his friend on the shoulder. Archie then crawled across the small confines and, like a contortionist, made his way through the small opening. He was now in his tool shed. The old coveralls were meticulously draped over the hook to hide his partner. The door was then quietly closed.

Now alone, the spy sat motionless in the bowels of the plant.

The damp coldness of the ancient structure enhanced its isolation. The pitch black darkness suspended his soul. It seemed that the pipes were holding him captive in a room where there was no escape. Like a commando behind enemy lines, he was in a dangerous situation and had to hide in silence.

Almost an hour had passed. The imprisoned employee was being neutralized to the confines of the dark room. Time stood still as thoughts about life now rushed through Matt's mind. He wondered what he actually was as a person. He was consumed by the stress of anticipation, curious about what he would hear. He began to question his value at the plant. Was he actually that great worker he thought he was? Did he really hold anyone's respect? The fear of the unknown continued as he pondered over the probability of this mission leaving him emotionally scarred- forever.

The solitude was interrupted by car doors opening and slamming shut. Seconds later, the smooth sound of a turning key was followed by the main office door opening. Heavy footsteps on the metal stairs increased in pitch as the secret party climbed the stairs to the second floor. The empty building created an echo chamber for the man in hiding. Then came a wicked sensation; the hollowed bayonets aimed at the intruder began to speak.

Conversations from the upstairs hallway passed through the pipes as another key could be heard turning a locks tumbler. The volume increased dramatically as the final door opened- then the evilness came! As noise was projected, the outdated pipes unmercifully amplified their sounds, blasting them into the secret dungeon. Years of wear allowed slight movement, causing the pipes to touch. An occasional chime from the barren metal would dance around the room when composure was lost. The unsystematic concussion from the invisible voices, and the ringing of lost emotions would seem endless. This scathe was just a fraction of the toll that would have to be paid.

"Jim, this will be the last time we'll meet like this," said a voice with authority. It was the unmistakable voice of the District Manager himself, Bruce Darby. Years of managing factories, union meetings, and smoking cigarettes had deteriorated his raspy vocal cords.

A dignified tone could then be heard, "We thought everything would be in control after our last meeting." The comment was from Jonathan Fields, the CEO of the entire corporation. "You have some explaining to do," he continued. Mr. Fields had a life of babysitting every plant. He was in constant travel with airports, hotels, and restaurants being "home." Having to come back to this factory was putting him over the edge.

A choked up supervisor replied, "We have made some progress here."

Bruce Darby angrily expressed, "You were supposed to have gotten rid of half the crew, including any troublemakers!"

"They've all been busy with plenty of work," defended Jim.

"That's because you keep them busy "finding" more work, yelled Bruce. "Times are hard; we have to cut back. This week, we even stooped low enough to have a meeting over your relations with Matt. He has the nerve to complain how you are keeping him employed- he doesn't get it. What we've created for him, he'll only protest. If we didn't try to bring in new work, he and others would have been gone years ago."

"You owe them nothing, Jim," said Jonathan Fields. "We can always replace you if that's what it takes!"

Jim quickly counter-punched. "Look," he said, "the company has been cutting back- a lot. My crew represents the best workers in this plant. They did more with less by taking on work from other departments. The extra men laid off in those areas exceed what I've held onto. We also did this without having to pay overtime. Plant wide, we're beyond our target at the expense of my crew." The room laid in silence for a minute as the deliberation continued.

"I guess I've never looked at it that way," said the composed CEO. "I still think Matt Berkley should be terminated."

"Mr. Fields," replied Jim, "he has taken on the brunt of these changes. He outworks everyone on a daily basis. He also gives this plant its highest attendance record. His effort motivates others to kick it up a notch and sets a vicious pace that others try to keep up with. Can you blame him for complaining? After all, he isn't aware of the plants status. Do you want him to know why things are so hard?"

"No," exclaimed Mr. Fields, "that would only cause panic throughout the plant. Is Matt actually a good guy?"

"Mr. Fields, he's the hardest worker I've ever known," stated the confident boss. "He's also a friend of over 25 years; I would trust him with my life."

"I see," said a calm Jonathan Fields. There was more silence between arguments as the fierce battle was coming to an end.

Matt Berkley's fists were clenched as his arms swung like a fan rooting for his favorite prize fighter. His boss would not go down in defeat! He almost yelled in support... until he remembered where he was.

"Okay, Jim," injected Bruce Darby, "you've bought more time. We are afloat now. Eventually, we will be forced to lay off more personnel, unless business picks up- a lot."

Then, the turning of a doorknob could be heard. It was followed by the mild squeak of door hinges. Descending footsteps echoed on the metal stairwell. The main door was opened and gently closed by itself.

A telephone ring could now be heard through the pipes. A relieved Jim Fairchild answers, "Hello?"

Through the intercom came the voice of Nancy Fairchild, "Are you still alive?" she asked laughingly.

"Yep, I'm still here," reported the husband.

"Can you explain the eight hundred dollars missing from our account?" she asked.

"You know what that is," answered Jim.

"Look, you have to stop doing this. The cutbacks took away all of the company bonuses. We don't even get anything! You never told the crew that there aren't any more Christmas bonuses. Instead, you cash out a vacation and give them one. Then you convince them it's from the company. The crew never gives you anything except headaches," said his upset wife.

"Nancy," paused the compassionate man, "it's Christmas. They work hard too. I do get paid a little more, and I want them to get at least something."

Then the most challenging aspect of the chamber came. Matt had to cover his face in an effort to muffle out his crying. He felt awful, realizing his boss's true life. It had never occurred to him the problems he actually gave that man. For this, could he ever forgive himself?

Nancy asked, "Did you accept the job?"

"Yes," he replied with enthusiasm. "I wanted that news to be a Christmas gift for you!"

"We've gone through so much pain; I needed the good news now," said a supportive Mrs. Fairchild. "When do you give notice?"

"January first," he replied. "We'll have a small New Year's party and tell our friends."

"Are you going to invite anyone from work?" she asked.

"Just Matt and Archie," said Jim. "We've been great friends through it all. Oh! What am I doing here? I'm supposed to be home with you! See you in a half hour honey; I love you!"

"I love you too," replied Nancy Fairchild.

The torture of truth was unbearable for Matt. He could only cover his ears and mouth to absorb the pain within. The love and respect for his old friend was rejuvenated. In silence, Matt spent the next twenty minutes shielding his ears from any sound. Moments later, Archie's flashlight beamed through the entrance of the vault.

"Matt," called out Archie, "they're all gone. I tried calling you on the phone. Are you all right?"

After a long pause, an exhausted Matt Berkley sighed in relief. In a tone of gratification, he said, "Now I understand what you were trying to tell me. A person can find Hell being where they shouldn't be. This was the most humbling experience I have ever had in my life. I also realize that I don't have it that bad after all." The free man threw off the blanket in disgust. He then crawled across the dirty pit to be released from its captivity. Outside, Archie could only look at him with soulful eyes. He too, had experience the Godforsaken reality in that very enclosure. It was a devastating experience of pain that they both now shared. Nothing would ever have to be said about it again.

The necessary tool needed to educate Matt Berkley had been employed. There was another long pause as he looked up at the stars, with the understanding of what he needed to learn. Matt was enlightened and exclaimed, "I feel great now!" The humbled working man looked at Archie and said, "Thank you; let's get something to eat!"

The lifelong friends shook hands and quietly left the grounds, keeping a well guarded secret.

# PETE'S WORLD

BRIAN STONE WALKED through the corridor that led to the mill. The automated sounds of augers turning, bucket elevators running, and white hot furnaces blasting made conversation impossible. The dejected employee felt that he was being placed on death row. He was on probation for failing the company's drug policy and demoted to a labor status. Usually, an employee was terminated at this stage of disciplinary action. He seemed, however, to be awarded a "standing eight count" in honor of his six year career. He was now being sent to "Siberia" for a final chance to save his job.

As he approached the metal reinforced door to the mill control room, he felt a presence. Beyond that barrier would be the most respected man in plant history, Pete Rainwater. This well-known legend ran the entire mill operation by himself - despite an entire work force of over one hundred men.

31

Pete was reliable. His territory covered half of the plant, including the lowest cavities and the highest perches. The irony of a punishment by being reassigned with the best gave Brian a peculiar feeling. He had to ask himself: "Why am I so lucky?" The most senior employees would gladly work with Pete if it were possible. The timid twenty-four year old grasped the steel lever, and with a mighty downward pull, he opened the heart of the plant and entered. The self-closing door concealed a quiet environment.

Sitting at the control panel was Captain Kirk himself: Pete Rainwater. His swivel chair was turned away from the console as he faced his new helper. This storied mill operator possessed an aura of respect. His grizzly bear stature was graced with the distinct facial features only known to the Native American. The spirited and warm character of a perceptive, wise, and understanding guru smiled in approval. The young laborer was overwhelmed to be alone with this icon in his element.

"Good morning, Brian," said Pete in a warm tone. "I asked to have you here for cleanup detail." A flattered Brian Stone was taken aback by the honor. Pete then said, "I'm worried about you."

The man looked in astonishment and asked, "Why?"

With authority, Pete said, "You were actually going to be terminated. I went to the office to find out why. They told me you aren't the same guy they hired six years ago. Their complaints ranged from a failed drug test, bad attendance, and poor job performance to a bad attitude about life in general. They were simply going to replace you with someone who cares. I asked if you could work with me for a while and get you back on track." Then, with soulful Pueblo eyes, the caring man asked, "What happened?"

Tears of shame started to run down Brian's face as he looked at the adult figure. "I went through a divorce last year, and I guess I stopped caring."

"But you still have a job!" replied Pete with firmness.

In gratitude, the broken co-worker hugged the giant man and replied, "Thank you."

The curator replied in a laughing manner. "So, let's keep that job!" Together they laughed, and then Pete showed him the areas that needed cleaning. A motivated Brian worked diligently on his assignments for the rest of the day.

The following morning, Brian showed up two hours late. His new boss was already hard at work in the refinery taking process temperatures of the huge furnaces. As the delinquent employee approached, Pete yelled above the noise. "Don't worry about it, I clocked you in on time; we can work this out later." The embarrassed laborer could only look in appreciation. The fatherly giant continued, "I brought us a lunch today, see you at noon." Brian smiled in relief, realizing that Pete knew of his economic status. Brian focused on an area until the lunch hour arrived.

The drudge was famished, and he entered the control room for lunch. Pete had fried chicken, potato salad, and corn for them. It was homemade from his kitchen, and was it ever good! Again, Pete took care of Brian as the young man devoured his meal.

Pete then asked, "How can you be late when you live alone?"

Brian said, "Women."

An inquisitive Pete asked, "What did you do last night?"

"I had a date," replied a smug Brian. "We were out late and drank too much."

"I thought that you had children?" questioned the concerned elder.

"I do, but they live with their mother," answered the young man.

"Then, how often do you see them?" inquired the boss.

With a long pause, Brian answered, "Not since Christmas."

"Why?" asked Pete.

Brain took another bite of chicken as he savored the much needed nourishment. He then answered, "They don't want to know me, just like their mother."

Pete stood up and looked straight at Brian. The large man said, "I'm glad you shared that with me; it's the furthest thing from the truth!" Pete was upset and immediately left the room to allow the information to sink in.

The work day continued with tension. The amateur therapist left Brian alone with his thoughts. The introverted expression on Brian's face was all Pete had to see. It illustrated the pain he was secretly going through. Brian was now in a safe haven. He was obviously brought there by Pete to survive his divorce and redirect his life. At quitting time, the man purposely gave Brian space. The thoughts going through his mind would consume him for a long time, with solitude being the best medicine.

The following morning gave tell-tale signs of Brian's troubled life. The faltering worker was late again. As he arrived three hours late, his spiritual safety net was there to greet him and provide more clemency.

"Relax," said Pete in a comforting tone. "The company is monitoring you through my reports. I tell them that you show up on time and work hard. All is fine, and you can make up the lost time later." Then he asked, "What's your excuse this time?"

The Casanova sat down and pondered where to start. "My girlfriend and I broke up. I got drunk again and missed the bus this morning."

His counselor asked a strategic question: "Why do you think she left?"

"Because nobody wants to be with a loser," answered the patient in a soft tone.

"What made her want you in the first place?" asked Pete.

"We both have children from past marriages," replied Brian. "We felt we could provide them a better home if we got together. She left after knowing me for only two months."

The elder asked, "Did you get along with her children?"

"Yes!" exclaimed Brian. "I did everything for them."

The adviser continued questioning. "Does she know your children?"

Brian's naive face contorted, and he quietly answered, "No."

Pete looked directly at Brain and said, "She's looking for a man to marry and showed you that her children come first. You showed her that only you come first. You weren't qualified to be a step-father because you aren't being a dad to your own children." The absent father tensed up with this realization, and he cried like a child. Pete left the room to resume his job.

Lunch time arrived one hour later. Pete provided another warm homemade meal. The zesty lasagna, garlic bread, and salad were fit for a restaurant.

Brian tasted the hardy meal and asked Pete, "How did you learn to cook like this?"

Pete sat back and stated, "I have been cooking my whole life. My children and their friends always asked to have dinner in our home. My grandchildren always want to have dinner with me. I even went to a culinary school to improve my skills. Unless I can share it with someone, it's a wasted art."

Brian thought for a moment, then remarked, "I thought your kids were raised and that you lived alone."

With a warm smile Pete said, "It seems that I have someone to cook for this week." Brian sat back in awe. He had the feeling that the best man he ever knew had adopted him!

"Now," resumed Pete, "tell me about your children."

With vivacity, the young father stood up and exposed his wallet. He opened it up and began to display their pictures. "These are my two girls! Beth is three, and this is my six year old, Janet."

Pete put on his reading glasses to review the pictures and commented, "They are very pretty."

"Thank you," responded Brian. He continued talking about his daughters for the next twenty minutes. On occasion, laughter would accompany the cute stories about them. A caring Pete listened intently and enjoyed the stories. Eventually, Brian changed tone and asked Pete for a big favor.

"Go ahead," Pete replied.

A reluctant Brian was behaving like a dog with its tail between its legs. He struggled to find courage, then asked a series of questions. "I heard that the mill will be down this Friday for maintenance work," remarked Brian.

An intrigued Pete looked at Brian and answered, "That's true."

Then the timid laborer asked if they were going to have the day off.

"We could," answered Pete.

Brian looked at Pete and asked, "Do you have plans this weekend?"

"No," he answered.

With a long face, Brian began to explain his situation.

37

"I have to attend Family Court for an arbitration hearing this Friday. This is to see my kids and to prove in court that I am qualified to be a father. This appointment is at nine o'clock in the morning at the courthouse in Cedar City. This is all the way in Redford County, and I have no way to get there."

Pete smiled and responded, "A road trip would do me good; let's have a three day weekend! We can leave Thursday night after work. That town has a hotel with a cafe. We can stay there and spend Friday together. You can even introduce me to your kids!"

Brian could only hug Pete as he shook with tears. Once again, Pete took care of him.

Medford County was a two hour drive. They devised a plan to have Pete pick up Brian in front of his apartment at four o'clock. The two would then drive to Cedar City and have dinner at the Pine Cone Hotel and Cafe. This would give Brian plenty of rest for his court appearance.

Pete arrived at Brian's apartment ten minutes early. The absent father was already waiting in the parking lot, empty handed. He wore the same clothes he had on the day before and had probably slept in them. He hadn't shaved that week, and his shirt was unbuttoned. The messy hair made the package complete.

Rolling down his window, Pete said, "Wrong!"

A puzzled Brian asked, "What do you mean by that?"

"Look at you!" exclaimed the drill sergeant. "You're going to face a judge and your children looking like that?

This is the most important job interview that you'll ever have; go get clean clothes, and look the part!"

Without hesitation, Brian ran back to his apartment and returned a few minutes later with a small travel bag. The out of breath junior said, "I will look the part tomorrow!"

"Much better," said Pete. "Now, let's go." The two comrades then embarked on their journey to Redford County. The pleasant ride provided a setting for friendly conversation. Brian even forgot about the seriousness of this trip. The tired men entered the Cedar City city limits about six o'clock.

The men were hungry when they arrived at the Pine Cone Cafe. A warm meal and lodging would be a great end for their busy day.

After being seated, a problem presented itself. The husband and wife team who owned and operated the small business had no cook. Their chef had to leave town moments earlier for a family emergency. The Wilsons were caught off guard and didn't know what to do.

An apologetic Mr. Wilson greeted the customers to share the bad news. "I am sorry for the inconvenience, but we don't have a cook tonight. We have no choice but to close the restaurant for the evening."

Pete then answered, "I'll have to disagree with that; you have a cook right here!" Pete's many years of cooking for others was enough experience for the challenge. The Wilsons were bewildered; they needed a cook immediately and were at Pete's mercy. They had no choice but to accept his offer and take the gamble. As Pete stood up to shake hands with the owners, he looked at Brian and said, "Life's calling!"

Then, with a look of determination, he was led to the kitchen.

The managers watched in awe as they saw Pete get familiarized with his new work station. With calm control, he asked, "Do you have a grocery store nearby?" The Wilsons nodded their heads up and down. "Great!" said the chef. "Do you have a blackboard with chalk?" The response was the same. "Fantastic!" exclaimed Pete. "Gather all of the menus, and I will write on the blackboard what the dinner choices are tonight. This will work out just fine!" Right away, he wrote out a grocery list and sent the couple to the store. Pete then wrote the dinner menu on the blackboard. The reader board read:

## Welcome to the Pine Cone Café

### Tonight's dinner choices are:

**Homemade lasagna with garlic bread**
**New York steak or fried chicken with mashed potatoes and gravy**
**All entrees come with salad or vegetable soup**

It was a stroke of luck that Pete and Brian were the first customers. The slow Thursday evening in the small town bought much needed time for Pete to organize his new surroundings. He quickly set up an assembly line to produce the dinner choices. He was in his element and happy to save the day. The Wilsons returned promptly with the groceries and were pleasantly surprised with the reader board that graced the lobby.

Moments later, the first customers arrived. They were senior citizens, and that bought more time for the busy cook because the couple only wanted soup and salad. Soon, pasta was baking, chicken was being fried, and mashed potatoes with rich country gravy were on the stove. A pot of soup stayed warm on the back burner, enhancing the aroma of the quaint cafe. A relieved husband and wife studied Pete's cooking skills and looked at one another in tears. They realized that his presence was a gift from up above.

Pete quickly prepared beautiful plates of salad and wholesome bowls of warm soup for the aging couple. It was attractive and tasted even better! The healthy meal was savored by the elders.

Soon, the dinner crowd began to arrive in small doses. Within the hour, the restaurant was full, with more customers arriving in the parking lot.

Pete was ready! The ingenious cook already had dinner prepared in mass quantities. It was now just a matter of Mrs. Wilson taking orders and Pete fulfilling them. They were ahead of the game! Mr. Wilson filled in the cracks as he washed dishes, bused tables, and kept all drinks filled. He even handled the cash register when his wife was busy serving their guests.

Brian was amazed with this harmony. He suddenly realized that he could also be of help. He could only empty garbage, keep fresh coffee brewing, and assist busing tables, but he contributed! Together, the four worked hard and survived the night. The shift seemed flawless, and everyone performed like clockwork. The busy restaurant never missed a beat! Time went by fast as hungry customers arrived in droves and left happy. The tips were testimony to the great excellence of this operation. The many compliments made the venture even better!

Closing time was delayed because of the many customers. At one time, it seemed that some of the diners would get on their cell phones to tell local friends about having dinner at the Pine Cone Cafe that night. The food and service was that great! Finally, the last table was cleared, and the sign that read "Closed" was placed on the cafe's locked front door. The lights that advertised an operation in business were dimmed. The weary foursome then got to sit down and have their dinner together. A variety of dishes were spread on the table closest to the kitchen. The Wilsons were now about to enjoy one of the greatest meals of their lives.

The feast began with an indebted Mr. Wilson placing a rolled up, undetermined amount of cash into Pete's shirt pocket. He then said that he and his wife had never been so lucky in their entire lives. "Please accept the money; it has been one of the best nights we ever had running this restaurant. All of us earned well tonight!" The grateful man then continued, "You will also stay here for free; it's the least we can do for you!" Pete was touched. He never expected anyone to pay him when he was able to do a favor. He respected the Wilsons' dignity, and for that reason only, he accepted their gifts.

Brian sat back and learned. The dinner was a Thanksgiving, with each person appreciating the other. Soon, Mr. Wilson led the tired travelers to their hotel room. With a sincere smile accompanied by a warm handshake, he said, "Please visit anytime, and thank you for helping us!"

In typical fashion Pete answered, "You're welcome, the

pleasure's mine!" It was almost 11:30, and the weary men needed much sleep. Pete washed up in the bathroom and dressed for bed. "Good night, Brian," he said in a fatherly voice, "I'll see you in the morning." Brian acknowledged Pete, and wished him the same. Pete turned off the lights, falling asleep within minutes. Brian could only stare at the dark ceiling and ponder about the day's events. He thought about the great man Pete was and wanted to be just like him.

It seemed that as soon as Brian fell asleep, he was being awakened by Pete. The dedicated man was already dressed, and the morning sunlight shined its rays across the room. "You have an hour and a half until your court appearance. We are only fifteen minutes away, and your breakfast is on the table." Brian looked at the room's lone table and saw a bowl of oatmeal, a banana, a cup of coffee, and a glass of orange juice.

"Thanks!" Brian said joyously, and he sat down at the table to eat.

"I'll be back in a half hour," said Pete as he left the room. Brian then showered, shaved, and got into the clean clothes he brought. As he was finishing his coffee, Pete returned. "You look good!" said the guardian in approval.

"I appreciate that; I don't want to make any mistakes today," replied a refreshed Brian.

"Good!" stated Pete. "Let's check out now and get there early."

When the two travelers reached the hotel desk, a noticeable coffee can for donations was on the counter. It had a picture of a seventeen-year-old girl and a description of her dream. Her name was Clare Wilson, a local high school student. Her family was trying to collect enough donations to afford a field trip to New York. This would allow her an audition to represent her county for the state beauty pageant. Brian noticed the container first but walked away.

Without any thought, Pete took the rolled currency Mr. Wilson had placed in his shirt pocket and forced the entire bundle through the thin opening on top of the can. It was obvious that Pete never counted the many bills. He believed in that child's dream, and that's all that mattered. More importantly, Pete didn't want anyone to know about his generous contribution. *He* was the only one who had to know—but had no idea that Brian saw this charitable act. The Wilsons would quickly figure out where that donation came from.

There was a reason why Pete had Brian leave early for an appointment only a few minutes away. The sage was going to use his wisdom to have the "father on trial" in the proper mind-set for this important evaluation. Once in the car, the wise father began to prime Brian for the courtroom. He started off by asking him how he felt about being divorced.

Brian's answer was bitter. "I didn't do anything wrong; she just wanted me to grow up. I felt that she wanted to be with someone else, anyway, and that I would find out about it sooner or later. When she kicked me out of our home, I felt that we were never a family in the first place. It bothered me to pay child support for a family that I wasn't allowed to be a part of. Why should I care at that point?"

Pete gave a long sigh in understanding and said, "That's how I felt when I divorced." Brian sat up in disbelief and wanted to hear more. The single dad continued, "When I divorced, my three children lived with their mother. It seemed that I was a stranger and that someone else would eventually take my place as their father. It was hard to pay money and not be as close as I wanted to be. At one time, I wondered if I should just move far away and sever all ties. One day, it occurred to me that I always carried their pictures, just as you do. When I started to talk about them, I couldn't stop, just like you. Those are my children, no matter what! I am their father, and only I can end that. I won't!" With a stern look on his face, Pete looked at Brian and asked, "Is that how you feel?"

Brian sat tall and yelled out, "That's exactly how I feel!"

Pete continued, "I also learned something about life. You don't have to be related to anyone to find happiness sharing with them. I always get to be myself whenever I want to. Nobody can stop me from being that!" Then he looked at Brian and asked, "Why don't you let your children—as well as everyone else—know who the real Brian is?" The wise man then extended his hand to shake Brian's, and with encouragement said, "Come on in, the water's fine!"

An inspired Brian yelled out, "I will! It will be for everyone, especially my kids!"

Pete then asked if there were any barriers that would prevent him from seeing his children again.

With confidence, Brian yelled out, "Only this!" He

pulled out of his pocket two thousand dollars. This was back child support to be paid to his former wife. It would show the court that he did have a job and was being responsible. Moments later, they arrived in front of the court house and were greeted by Brian's case worker. The young father left the car and looked at Pete saying, "I'm ready!"

Pete smiled and responded, "Yes, you are! I'll be waiting in the lobby for you." It was twenty minutes before his appearance as Brian entered the building with his councilor.

Pete now had an indefinite amount of alone time. He casually got out of his car and walked the beautiful grounds. There were well manicured paths that led to a rose garden, several ponds accompanied by ducks, and breathtaking views of the valley. Eventually, he entered the court house and leisurely admired its rustic beauty. Soon, he found his way to the lobby, and sat in a comfortable leather chair. At random, he selected a magazine and began to read. The quiet relaxation of enjoyable reading found Pete lost in time.

The tranquility was abruptly interrupted when the courtroom doors swung open. The lobby was now full of the happy sounds that only children could make. Pete looked towards the commotion and saw a very happy man with two happy girls. It was Brian!

"Hey, you wanted to meet them!" exclaimed Brian. Then he introduced the daughters to his hero. The girls sat on Pete's lap and hugged him as if he were Santa Claus!

Then, a woman's voice could be heard. "You must be Pete! I am Shelly, Brian's former wife. We have heard many good things about you. Brian told us that you have been taking great care of him and brought him to us. We want to thank you for helping our family; he was missed by all of us!"

Pete smiled, and with a teary eye said, "The pleasure is all mine!" He then received a warm hug from Shelly as Brian shook his hand. The grateful mother opened her purse and pulled out a package wrapped in tinfoil accompanied with an envelope. With a caring voice, she called out to the daughters and asked them to give Pete his gift. The children took the present from her and presented it to Pete.

The large man was touched and opened up the card first. It was made by the girls and had hand imprints inside, along with a multicolored message of thanks. Pete's eyes opened wide when he unwrapped the package and discovered homemade cookies. "I love cookies!" cried out the loving man. The scene immediately broke into a group hug!

"We are going to have a picnic at a local park and stay the night at Shelly's home. We'd love to have you!" said Brian. "Shelly is even willing to drive me back home tomorrow!"

Pete looked with satisfaction and said, "Well, good! It looks like you have some catching up to do. I need to get back home now; I have some chores to finish. I'll see you at work on Monday."

Then, the saintly man stood up and hugged Brian like a bear saying, "I am proud of you!" Pete said his good-byes to the reunited family and left the building. They watched attentively as the graceful soul walked through the parking lot with the gifts, entered his car, and began the long drive home.

There was now a calm presence that surrounded the young family. They felt a unity that would always be protected by Pete's love and strength. As he traveled out of sight, they embraced one another with a bond of security.

Walking hand in hand with Shelly, the revived father watched his children play on the vast grounds of the courthouse. He looked up at the afternoon sky and thought about Pete. He wondered if the good Samaritan might stop at a small-town cafe somewhere for lunch, or find a stranded motorist who needed his assistance. Thoughts continued to race through his mind as he tried to imagine whose path Pete would cross next and how many lives would be touched.

# LITTLE JEFFREY AND THE BIG FACTORY

IT WAS JEFFREY HOLDEN'S first day on the job...again.

As he approached the main doors of the factory, he wondered how long he would last at this job. It seemed that Jeffrey never got along with anyone he worked with, but in his mind, it was never *his* fault. He felt that everyone he had ever worked with didn't respect him and were always teasing him. He believed they looked down at him as a child who wasn't capable of doing his job.

His new environment seemed to predict the future. It was just another Gothic structure made out of metal and brick. Dull steel doors that enclosed the plant gave a cold, unwanted feeling. This could only be an institution that would force him to sacrifice life for survival, a prison that offered no freedom.

Just then, Jeffrey was startled by a friendly voice.

"Well, hello there," greeted a senior gray-haired man. "You must be Jeffrey Holden! My name is Bill Hansen; I will be your new supervisor. We are happy to have you here. Let me know if there is anything I can do for you!"

Jeffrey muttered a quiet "Thank you," shaking hands with his new boss.

"I have worked here for over twenty years, and I guarantee that you will like it here!" exclaimed Bill.

"I am happy to hear that," replied the soft-spoken young man.

"We always begin our shift with a crew meeting," said Bill. "I'll introduce you to the guys."

He led the new employee to the break room. Jeffrey's stomach had knots in it. He had never gotten along with his co-workers before, so why would this be any different?

The workers were already present when Bill and Jeffrey entered. A jubilant Bill Hansen greeted the room. "Good morning! I'd like to introduce you to our newest member; this is Jeffrey Holden!"

Immediately, there was a warm reception for Jeffrey. Then, each member introduced himself and shook his hand. Jeffrey's small stature made him feel uncomfortable as his new workmates towered over him.

"Pleased to meet you, Jeffrey, my name is Hong Lee!"

"Good Morning, Jeffrey, I'm Pete Rainwater!"

"Welcome aboard, Jeffrey, Steve Williams is the name!"

A timid Jeffrey responded with a polite, "Thank you, I'm glad to meet everyone."

The morning meeting was brief and covered the day's assignments.

"Hong, let's start off this morning with you giving Jeffrey a tour of our shop," suggested Bill.

"It will be my pleasure!" replied Hong.

He led the new member to the shop and began to show him the various work stations. Then, it happened. Hong was showing Jeffrey the safety equipment cabinet. Once he began explaining which items had to be worn in the shop, Jeffrey barked back, saying, "Do you think I'm stupid? I know to wear safety gear on the job!"

Hong was shocked at Jeffrey's response and anger. "I was just showing you where the safety gear is and what we need for the job," replied Hong in defense.

"I don't need you to tell me things I already know!" shouted Jeffrey.

"Look, Jeffrey," said Hong with diplomacy, "let's have Pete show you around."

"Fine!" he snapped back.

Pete was then summoned to continue the tour. It didn't take Jeffrey long to lose his temper again. Pete started to show Jeffrey how to operate the drill press when he was interrupted with an insult.

"Do you really think I don't know how to operate that drill?"

51

"There seems to be a problem here," replied Pete in a calm voice. "Do you want to address our supervisor about what's making you so upset?"

A frustrated Jeffrey Holden lashed out, "I will!" He then marched off to Bill Hansen's office.

It was morning break as the crew assembled in the break room. Pete and Hong were dismayed that Jeffrey was so quick tempered on the job. They each shared their morning experiences.

"I also had a problem with Jeffrey today," explained Steve. "This morning before work, I allowed him to enter the parking lot before I did. It seems we both arrived at the exact same time. He got upset and shouted at me saying, "I am not an old lady, I can take care of myself!" I knew that he must have been our new employee. I didn't want to jeopardize his job, and that's why I didn't tell anyone about it."

Mr. Hansen then entered the room, but he was alone. He announced to the crew that after a brief visit with Jeffrey, he sent him home. "I told him that the crew is well proven and that he needs to get along with everyone to work here. He is allowed to come back tomorrow if he's willing to try."

"Jeffrey has a problem," said Hong. "Maybe we can find out what it is and help him."

"Hong's right!" yelled Pete. "We need to get to the bottom of this!"

"I agree!" said Steve. "Maybe he can correct himself and save his job; it's worth a try."

"Fellas, I'm proud of you!" said an inspired Bill Hansen.

"How did Jeffrey get hired in the first place?" asked Pete.

"Well...his aunt works in accounting. She asked if we could hire her nephew. It seems he has a problem holding a job. Brenda has worked for us a long time, and I agreed to give him one chance," explained Bill.

"Let's talk to Brenda after work," suggested Steve. "We can all be there and hopefully, we can reach an understanding."

"Agreed!" said the room in unison.

The crew resumed their work as Bill arranged a meeting with Brenda. They met in the break room after work.

The meeting started off with Brenda apologizing for her nephew's behavior. She admitted that Jeffrey had a problem that needed to be understood. Each crew member then explained about the conflict they had. The meeting, however, was about their concern for Jeffrey's welfare.

"Brenda, you told us that Jeffrey has a history with this problem," stated Pete. "What is the problem, anyway?"

Brenda leaned back in her chair and said, "Okay...this is what the problem is. He has a complex based on his physical stature."

"You mean a 'Little Man Complex'?" inquired the

supervisor.

"Yes," replied Brenda.

"No one has made any comments about Jeffrey's height," exclaimed Hong. "Nobody has insulted him!"

"Maybe not by your standards," said Brenda. "Jeff was always the shortest boy in class and at every job he held. He believes that others underestimated him based on that. When you are friendly to him, are you *too* friendly? Do you ever talk to him the way an adult addresses a child? Do you offer too much help for him, but not others? There is also something I don't understand. Why do you refer to him with a child's name? His friends call him 'Jeff' and never anything else."

The room was silent. The crew didn't realize that they were treating Jeff differently. It never occurred to them how condescending they were to their new co-worker.

"It's time to treat Jeff like an adult!" stated Steve.

"Agreed!" cried out the crew.

"Starting tomorrow, this supervisor will treat Jeff like a man!" proclaimed Bill Hansen.

The following morning, Jeff parked his car next to Pete's. "Good Morning, Jeff," acknowledged Pete.

Jeff stopped in amazement. It was a happy sound to be called by his real name! "Hey, you too, Pete!" responded Jeff.

Pete walked to the plant with a big smile on his face.

"Jeff, I need to talk to you." It was Mr. Hansen with a stern look on his face. "Our company is re-structuring. According to your resume, you have experience in receiving raw materials. We need a new system that will unite the entire company when merchandise is needed immediately. Are you up for the task?"

Jeff loved the moment! He was now being assigned a very important responsibility. What made it even better was that he got to do it his way. He would be working alone and acting as his own boss. This was Jeff's opportunity to prove himself. "Mr. Hansen," exclaimed Jeff, "I promise that I will not let you down!"

"Great!" said the proud elder. "You will be given everything you need for this project. Let me show you our aging storeroom."

He led Jeff to the back of the factory. They soon arrived at the oldest part of the plant. It still had the original shelving, lighting, and paint. Everything was dusty and dirty in the dim environment.

"Do you think you can help us here?" asked the challenging boss.

Jeff could only look in excitement as he thought about the vast improvements he could make. The enthused employee broke out of his trance and said, "Yes, sir!"

"You can start immediately," said Mr. Hansen.

Jeff started the arduous task by working through his first break. He continuously thought of better ways to organize the old storeroom and implement a new system. The enlightened employee dedicated himself to this project and was willing to work extra hours.

Several weeks went by. Then, one morning, Jeff reported to Mr. Hansen's office. "Job's all done, sir!" exclaimed Jeff.

Mr. Hansen was shocked. He was curious to see what Jeff had actually accomplished. "The entire plant wants to see what you have done with the old storeroom. Everyone noticed the long hours you have put into this project. We are all aware how hard you have worked on it," said the intrigued supervisor. "Do you object to giving a presentation after lunch?"

"Not at all," said a confident Jeff Holden. "In fact, that's a good idea!"

Mr. Hansen was impressed; Jeff had never paid anyone at work a compliment before! "Very well," responded the boss. "I will notify everyone in the plant to meet at the store room at noon today."

"I'll be ready!" Jeff replied.

Shortly after lunch, a line began to assemble at the storage room entrance. There were noticeable improvements already made. The old hallway was clean and freshly painted. There was even a small waiting area with chairs and a matching table. Plants in attractive pots along with tasteful wall hangings graced the waiting room. For the first time in company history, a sign reading 'Storeroom' had been hung outside above the door.

At twelve o'clock, the storeroom door opened. A smiling Jeff Holden stood tall and greeted the masses.

The crowd was eager to see what else Jeff had improved. With Bill Hansen and Brenda Holden leading the way, Jeff announced, "Please enter!"

As the work force entered the storeroom, there was an immediate silence. The beauty from the hallway continued. The old, run-down room had been renovated. It was no longer a dark and dirty eye sore. It was clean with fresh paint and had plenty of lighting! The front counter had a catalog that gave simple instructions for the new procedure. Jeff had ingeniously suspended from the ceiling a numerical system going one way along with an alphabetical system going another. Together, any item could now be pin-pointed within the room. There was also a log book that recorded whenever anything arrived or was issued out. This was a simple, flawless procedure that even a child could do!

The old storeroom was now a masterpiece! When Jeff finished his presentation, he asked if there were any questions. There were no questions to be asked; all was completely understood!

Then came the greatest moment in Jeff Holden's life: the entire room gave him an ovation! The cheering from his fellow workers lasted several minutes in recognition of his accomplishment. For the first time in his life, Jeff had been acknowledged for being intelligent! The smile on his face was proof! Jeff was now getting a little embarrassed and said, "Thank you, I really appreciate this!"

The new employee began to love his job. He made a name for himself with the storeroom project. The waiting room he created was now a popular meeting place for friends. This allowed him to be introduced the way he wanted to be.

He also changed in character. Before, he was defensive, but now, he seemed to like everyone— including himself! Jeff was no longer the stranger that complained about everything; he now appreciated everyone. He was starting to help others and was willing to learn from them. It seemed that Jeff Holden finally found a job that he could call home.

Then, one morning, Jeff's aunt met him in the parking lot. "Mr. Hansen wants to see you first thing this morning," said Brenda.

Jeff's heart sank as he felt a lump in his throat. Usually, such a meeting was when he would get fired. Those moments were always anticipated. Most of the time, he hated the job so much that he *wanted* to get fired, except for the times when he just walked off. However, his recent success made him grateful for what he had. Now, he was happy and felt accepted. The determined employee made a beeline to his supervisor's office. Mr. Hansen's door was already open.

"Good morning, Jeff. We need to talk," said Bill.

Jeff sat down and pleaded to save his job. "Mr. Hansen, you need to know I have changed as a person! I like it here just as you told me I would. I admit that I have handled some things wrong, but that was the *old* me. I want to stay here! I like everyone! I don't care what my assignments are, just as long as I can work here!"

"Calm down, Jeff," interrupted Bill. "You are not being fired; the company wants to offer you a new position! You have done a spectacular job with the old storeroom and gave a professional presentation. You have made this company more resourceful and efficient! The corporate heads were inspecting the plant this weekend and were impressed with your new system. They were down-sizing this plant, along with our affiliates. When they saw what we now have, a decision was made to make our storeroom the central location for all our plants. The room to consolidate this surplus now exists here. A full time job has been created by expanding this department.

"We all agreed that the title should go to the person who created it. This one-man operation belongs to none other than Jeff Holden." The seasoned boss then offered sound advice. "Take it, Jeff. This is a beautiful world you created, and it's ever better with you in it."

Jeff was overwhelmed! He never imagined that he could love a job. He was surprised that by applying himself, he could create a dream job of his own. The thought of running an operation by himself and contributing to all the plants was beyond his wildest dreams. He also welcomed the many friends who would visit him and share their breaks in the surroundings he provided. He could hardly speak and was actually shaking over the shock of success. After a long pause, he quietly stammered, "Yes, I'll accept that position." A humble Jeff Holden then shook hands with his supervisor.

"I was expecting you to reach that decision," said a happy Bill Hansen. "Now follow me."

Mr. Hansen led Jeff to the break room. The room was decorated with banners congratulating him. Brenda was waiting there and presented her nephew with a large cake. Jeff was fighting back the tears when he read the inscription: "JOB WELL DONE!"

Once again, Jeff received a standing ovation as his newly acquired friends shook his hand. Cake, soda pop, and ice cream contributed to this great social gathering. Laughter was shared as everyone visited the guest of honor, praising his work.

It was now Jeff's turn. He positioned himself toward the crowd and got their attention. "Thanks, you guys," exclaimed the emotional hero. "I wouldn't be here if you didn't give me a chance. You saw through my flaws and realized that I could actually be good at something. I'm aware that everyone had to cope with me and that I had to change. When I was assigned this project, everyone supported me—I needed that! You allowed me to find myself. I am now the 'Jeff Holden' I was meant to be, and I love it here! Please visit me in the storeroom whenever you can!"

The room cheered in approval as Jeff confirmed a family status with the company. Soon, the half hour celebration came to an end with everyone returning to their work stations. With pride, a motivated Jeff Holden marched to his very own department and started his new job.

# THE EAST SIDE BROTHERHOOD

CODY BROWNE peacefully entered the conference room. The quiet tension emphasized the importance of this meeting. His three-year career was, once again being challenged in the company judicial system. The combination of poor attendance and twice failing a random drug test brought him to trial. This makeshift court consisted of his supervisor, plant manager, and head of the Human Resource Department. They were waiting for the defense to arrive: his shop steward and union representative.

Dark circles surrounding brown eyes showed signs of self-inflicted abuse. Light-faded green tinted skin accompanied his unkempt long brown hair. An overgrown handlebar mustache blended with his rebellious character.

Cody sat down and looked at the long faces viewing him. All knew why he was here. Finally he spoke out,

"What do you want from me?"

Phil Smith, the Plant Manager responded, "This Company feels that you have violated too many policies. When you called in sick last Friday, you again exceeded the amount of sick days allowed within the year. We have given you many chances to save your job. We are fed-up and throwing in the towel. We don't like doing this anymore than you do."

Without hesitation, the defiant thirty-six year old said, "Then what are you waiting for?"

The large man in stature pointed out, "It's your legal right to have union representation."

The cocky employee stated, "I don't need them; they have never done anything for me! How about I quit? That would make things easier." Cody stood up with a smug expression and announced, "I quit!" He then left the room, seemingly without a care in the world. The remaining staff could only look at one another in pity.

The November wind had a chill in the air as he left the plant for his long walk home. The meeting had no affect on his conscious. However, returning home during working hours did. The man lived with his mother and losing another job would only escalate the already troubled home life. He approached the house he grew up in and cautiously entered through the back door.

The fifty-eight-year-old woman on social security saw him. She was in the kitchen baking bread as her morning was interrupted. The expression on her face did not require any words. She was once again playing the role of a disappointed truant officer. It was obvious that there could only be one reason to see her son arriving home during that time of day. She quietly continued her project. Cody went to his room and left the house moments later.

The American town of Southfork was small. One could actually walk anywhere in town and reach their destination within an hour. What this community lacked in casinos, five-star hotels, and high-rises, was made up in unity. This was that small town where everyone seemed to know everybody. Holidays were special and always celebrated on a grand scale. Street decorations and parades were dedicated to each day observed. The main job in town was the flour mill that served half the country. A grocery store, theater, small shops, and a few diners balanced out the business district.

There was also a famous resident in the area: "The East Side Brotherhood." They were a nationally acclaimed group of good men that served their community. The Brotherhood worked closely with local churches, community services, and the police. They filled in the gaps where help was needed. Poverty stricken families could take up shelter, and a warm meal was always offered. Preachers would give sermons every night of the week. Their doors were always open, with everyone welcomed.

Cody braved the freezing winds as he walked down the desolate street. The closest place of refuge was a neighborhood tavern called, "Sam's Place." The unemployed man entered the empty bar and sat alone. He then addressed the owner and asked, "Can I put this on my tab?"

An angry bartender barked back, "Now Cody, you have had one for several years - still unpaid!"

"Sam," replied Cody in defense, "I'll pay up soon!"

"How can you?" asked the small business man. "You just lost another job; the words all over town! I don't want your money! All you have to do is leave and never come back!" The outcast then looked down to digest the rejection. He then left without saying a word.

The lone man buttoned up his coat to stay warm. The day was getting colder and sunset would bring frost. As the pariah left the bar, he wondered where to go. The small town had gambled on him so many times and never won. He seemed to be painted in a corner where the unconditional love of family was all that was left. In despair, he chose a path that would lead to his sisters and brother-in-law's house. He prayed that they would still accept him and provide shelter. Nightfall was arriving as the brother slowly climbed the stairs, leading to the front door.

His older sister, Susan, must have anticipated her predictable brother's arrival. She opened the door before he had a chance to knock on it. In a calm tone, she said, "Your dinner is in the kitchen, and your room is ready." She led him to the kitchen and said, "Have a good night."

The down-and-out, broken man was humbled and could only say, "Thanks." The large helping of spaghetti with salad and garlic bread fed his hunger. He washed down the delicious meal with the milk provided. Quietly, the guest retreated to the familiar room that was always there for him. He was completing another day of not starting life. Cody was grateful to God that he still had family to save him, but, for how long? Eventually, "all good things come to an end."

The upstairs bedroom had a view of the valley. Snow began to fall as white flakes covered the neighborhood and foothills. The tired man was where he needed to be: sheltered with a warm meal. He let go of the day's anxiety and soon fell asleep.

When he awoke, it was an hour before dawn. He immediately dressed and left the house to conceal his presence. In shame, he wandered back to his mother's residence. Upon arriving, the disabled woman, with her hair in curlers, hugged the boy and began to make breakfast. Long ago, she learned to never point out the problems in his life. She was aware that they both knew his downfalls and to make an issue would only cause another fruitless argument.

Cody was well aware how fortunate he was to have his mother and sister. He understood that they wouldn't always be able to save him and that he had to address his life – once again. The problem child was getting old and had to do something "now." There was no choice but to dedicate this day to find work. After the nourishing meal, he bathed and walked to town looking for a future.

His first stop would be the unemployment office. Cody was first in line when the doors opened, and within twenty minutes he finished registering for his benefits. The rest of the day was to be spent beating the streets- looking for work. The town was entering the slow time of year, and no jobs were available.

Aimlessly, the cold and hungry man walked the sidewalks peering through the windows of restaurants.

He was hoping to recognize anyone that might offer him a seat at their table. All he saw was happy families enjoying their evenings. In depression, the street urchin continued his unorthodox travel...looking for anything.

Suddenly, a friendly voice called out his name. He looked across the street and was happy to see Tommy Wilson. He was the janitor at work who always had a pleasant smile for everyone. The stubby Irish man always said, "Hello," even to Cody.

"HI Tommy," shouted the former co-worker.

"Have you had dinner yet?" asked Tommy.

The question was another prayer being answered; Cody was starving. "No, I haven't," came the reply.

"My fellowship is having a dinner with a guest speaker; why don't you come with me," he suggested.

The straggler was relieved to have somewhere to go. It was a happy feeling that someone other his family was including him! "I'd love to," said the desperate man. Tommy then motioned him over to his car and opened the passenger side door.

"This will be a treat for you," said the happy custodian.

The luxury of a warm car to sit in and the company of a non-bias person were just short of a miracle. Once the car began driving down the road, Tommy expressed his condolences about Cody losing his job. He then gave encouragement that he would find another one and do fine.

The passenger appreciated the good man's compassion. He then asked, "Where are we going?"

"The East Side Brotherhood," exclaimed the driver.

That answer struck a nerve. "I won't go there," stated the arrogant Cody.

"Why?" asked the charitable man.

"I don't like those places," he answered in defiance. The vehicle rounded the final corner and pulled into the Brotherhood parking lot. Cody got out of the car and began to walk away.

"You are still welcomed; they'd love to have you," exclaimed Tommy.

But the stubborn man continued to walk away and said, "Thanks anyway."

Cody was well aware of the East Side Brotherhood. As a child, his family depended heavily on them for school clothes, food, and even an occasional Thanksgiving dinner. He was embarrassed when he got older. He hated his friends and classmates seeing his family receiving help from the Brotherhood. It hurt his pride and made him feel like a second-rate citizen. With these feelings, his only care was to walk away and keep walking.

Eventually, he reached the town's last remaining structure that signified a boundary line. It was a cobblestone bridge that was built during the Great Depression. It arched across a body of water called "Hobo Creek." This got its name from the many hobos that actually lived under the bridge during those hard times.

This historical monument also had a tragic significance. It was the last hope for many souls that traveled the country looking for work. In despair, countless numbers have taken their lives by jumping off the bridge into the unforgiving waters below. Its violent current promised death for those who gave up on life.

Cody always had knots in his stomach whenever he crossed this bridge. This is where two of his friends had taken their lives, not too long ago.

He stood alone at mid-span watching the rushing icy waters underneath him. He looked down stream into the darkness it traveled through. He paused to pray for the many souls that spent their final moments where he was standing.

Cody was much stronger than that. He also knew how to survive. It was time to reason with himself and make a good decision.

He had to swallow his pride. If he left now, he might make it back to the hall in time to have dinner. Anything was worth delaying his return back home. The frosty night began to freeze his ears and tired feet as he walked back to the East Side hall. Soon it was in sight. The rustic log cabin had smoke billowing out of its chimney. Snow covered the roof and ice cycles drooped down from the gutters. The windows had candles lit with the glass showing dampness of heat from the activities inside.

It was a warm holiday setting on a cold night. An oasis surrounded by a life-threatening climate. The tired traveler approached the heavily fortified front door and used its iron door knocker to request entry. Lifting the heavy weight and letting go, a loud concussion shook the door and signaled his arrival.

The fortress was opened by a large bearded man that graciously invited Cody inside. He introduced himself as "Brother Michael" and welcomed the transient.

The heat from the room wrapped around the destitute man, as the smell of alder wood and good food enticed him to enter. Like arriving at "Oz," everything that was needed seemed to be there. Brother Michael escorted the welcomed guest to a bench closest to the fireplace.

Then Cody caught a radiant smile from across the table. It was Tommy Wilson greeting his neighbor by saying, "I am glad that you could make it!"

A delicious aroma could be smelled as a bowl of warm stew was served to the late arrival. Sourdough rolls with butter and milk were also provided. Cody placed his jacket on a coat rack near the fireplace. Leaning forward, cold hands were exposed to the flames as moving fingers gained circulation. Now, it was dinnertime. Again, Cody was rescued.

He devoured the manna and was served a second portion. Upon finishing dinner, hot cider and cookies were offered to everyone in the room. Cody was warm, dry, and fed. He was, however, still like a cat: you could feed it- but wouldn't allow to pet. The moment a preacher took center stage to talk, Cody got his coat and quietly left. The Brotherhood was simply a "port in a storm." The loner would now brave the night once again and see if he still had a house to go to.

As he walked, thoughts about the day's events raced through his mind. He couldn't find a job, ran out of town, and had to rely on charity to help him survive another day. Worst of all, he was reminded of a last resort that others took when their lives had nothing. The disappointing son walked past empty parks, playgrounds, and schools that were once a security. It was almost eleven thirty at night when he walked the alleyway that led to the back doorsteps of his childhood. To his relief, the porch light was on signaling that the key was where his tired mother always hid it. He found it and quietly entered the warm abode.

The following morning, Cody awoke to the smells of a hearty breakfast. He dressed and hurried downstairs into the kitchen.

"Good morning, son," greeted his mother. The scrambled eggs, bacon, and hot cereal were a feast. The caregiver then served coffee and joined him at the breakfast table.

As the hungry man began to eat, he asked a question. "Mom, what do you think about the East Side Brotherhood?"

"They are the reason why we are still here," she replied.

"What do you mean?" asked the inquisitive son.

"When your father died, I had to start working," explained the widow. "I could only get minimum wage jobs and often got laid-off. They would pay our utilities and make sure we had food in the refrigerator. They have even gone as far as paying our mortgage so that we wouldn't lose our home. School clothes, Christmas gifts, and many other things were covered by those guys. Last night, they called to let me know that you were safe and being fed. That's more respect and consideration then you ever give us! You will always be taken care of by your sister and me because of the way they have taken care of us! If a family is "out," they do something about it. They have saved this whole town! In one way or another, everyone has been helped by them.

Cody leaned back in thought and then remarked, "I thought that they were just charity for the lower half."

"No, son," stated the mother. "They are what this town is famous for; the entire nation knows who they are! They are a special group of men that do things for this community that no other organization can. Everyone views them as celebrates and heroes! In fact, many have volunteered to be a member: doctors, lawyers, politicians, and even rich people! They can only give donations and visit their hall. Only a special breed is asked to be a member. To be a member in that Brotherhood is the highest level of success anyone could ever achieve. They are a one-of-a-kind!"

Cody could only sit back and let the rude awakening register. Tears of regret began to flow from his eyes as the truth penetrated his heart. He realized that it was his time to care and stop feeling sorry for himself. He was no longer going to complain and be a parasite to his family and community. It was now time to contribute. The aging son finished his breakfast and returned to his room. Within moments, he came back downstairs and cheerfully said, "Good-bye, mom," giving her a hug. He then left the house to visit where he had dinner the night before.

When Cody arrived at the lodge, several brothers were outside shoveling snow off the sidewalks. One of them was Brother Michael. Cody approached the burly God-fearing man and said, "I want to thank you for dinner last night."

Brother Michael recognized him and remembered his name. "You are very welcome, Cody. Everyone was glad that you were with us!"

"Let me help you with that," said Cody. He then took the snow shovel out of the big man's hands and proceeded to clear the sidewalk.

"Why, thank you," said the holy man.

"Let me know what else I can do," exclaimed the ambitious volunteer. "I have all day!" The other brothers were smiling in approval as they watched him work. Soon, all sixteen brothers were surrounding him.

"It's time to get acquainted," said Brother Michael. Then each brother extended his hand to Cody and introduced himself.

"Let me work with you guys all day," exclaimed Cody. The brothers all looked at one another in approval. They liked Cody! When he finished the sidewalk detail, he received compliments. It was now lunchtime, and the new helper was included.

The men surrounded their guest and cordially maintained a conversation. Cody felt good and had high self-esteem. Eventually, questions about his childhood were asked. They were pleased that he was from Southfork. Then one brother asked what his favorite childhood memory was growing up in that community.

Without any thought, he yelled out, "Christmas morning! Every year, Santa came down the street in his sled being pulled by a horse. I use to jump on it and ride on it down the block! He gave out candy canes and gifts! Sometimes, if there wasn't enough snow there were wheels on the sled!"

The brothers smiled in silence; then Michael spoke up. He asked Cody to follow him, and they left the room. They walked to a utility shed, and Michael opened it up. Cody looked inside and was in a state of shock. There was the red sled he used to ride on every Christmas morning! This discovery confirmed the many great moments his life had, thanks to the Brotherhood. Emotions were triggered as Cody cried in gratitude.

He then looked up at Brother Michael and said, "Thank you." Michael hugged Cody and left him alone to absorb the lesson. The East Side Brotherhood wanted Cody Browne to know exactly what they stood for. Cody soon returned to the hall and sat with the group. Looking at the members, he said, "What a childhood you guys gave me! You also took care of the family when we needed help. What can I do for the Brotherhood?"

"Cody," asked one of the elders, "we are going to ask a favor of you."

"Anything," he replied.

"We have a program called "Lifeguard." This is an effort to reach out to youth in the county jail. We listen and try to direct them to community services that will help with their problems. Many are drug and alcohol related; some come from bad home lives and need a positive change. We feel that you can talk to these teenagers and get results. We will spend the rest of the day at the county jail in honor of this program. Will you join us?"

Cody sat up in attention. His smile already gave the answer as he said, "Yes- I'd love that!" This was the first time in his life he was recruited for anything worthwhile! The band of Good Samaritans then gave him an ovation and shook his hand in acceptance. They coordinated to meet in the parking lot in five minutes. From there, they would board the Fellowship van and drive to the county jail. It was agreed that Cody would handle the first case.

The East Side Brotherhood arrived at the county jail within twenty minutes. When they entered the main lobby, the entire staff of police, secretaries, and visitors greeted them with open arms.

Moments later, they were given a police escort to a holding cell. The Brothers' watched in amazement as Cody recognized Justin Wright- a friend's younger brother. It was obvious that Justin idolized his older brother's popular friend. Cody then listened to the youth's problems and, with compassion directed him to visit his friends at the East Side Brotherhood.

He assured Justin that there were many great choices he would be able to make for his life – just as Cody did. He promised that he would be introduced to new friends that really did care and offered help.

The adolescent was full of joy and hope. He was invited by none-other than Cody Browne himself, to begin a new life - a better life. The ten minute consultation resulted in a warm emotional hug between the inmate and Cody.

Justin made his hero promise that he would visit him every day until he was released on probation. Cody gave his word that he would visit every day. He would keep that promise. With inspiration, he continued the crusade talking to each troubled youth that was behind bars. They all knew him and would accept his guidance anywhere. He gave sound advice and took time to thoroughly listen to their problems. Like Cody, they wanted to discover the East Side Brotherhood. They wanted to belong, just like him.

The ride back to the hall was silent. Everyone present was overwhelmed with what Cody had accomplished.

When the van entered the parking lot, the traditional open-dinner was underway. Cody immediately raced to the kitchen to assist. He served food, cleaned tables, sat hungry neighbors to their seats, and stoked the fire. All could see the pride inside this man! When the guests were served, he cleaned the army size pots and pans that fed many.

Then, the highlight of the evening came as Pastor Adrian began to preach.

Cody stopped working to sit in front of the congregation and listened. The pastor began a talk about feeding one another and caring. Cody was captivated by the holy man's message. For the first time in his life, Cody allowed a preacher to reach out to him and absorbed God's word. He listened to the message that encouraged them to look around and be grateful for what they had and to count their blessings.

Cody looked around the room. He saw the families that came to the hall receive a much needed warm meal. He looked at each Brother – and the loving look they had to serve God's will. The harmony in the log cabin was the greatest moment of peace Cody ever felt in his entire life. There were over forty people that joined the fellowship that evening. Together, they were a family.

Cody then had a revelation: he wasn't receiving anymore; he was contributing. It was the most respect he ever had for himself! He didn't want anything except to continue life on this path. When Pastor Adrian finished his sermon, Cody began to clap and soon the entire room gave an ovation! When the hall began to empty, the enlightened man went back to work. He was emptying garbage, straightening the long benches that sat the hungry, cleaning, and sweeping the polished wooden floors.

Cody was then confronted by the Brotherhood's Chairman, Ben Sampson. "The Brotherhood is requesting a meeting with you. We want to meet you by the fireside at eleven o'clock tonight; will you be there?"

A nervous Cody said, "Sure." He wondered if he overstayed his welcomed. Maybe bad experiences from his past had surfaced, and he was being asked to leave. He continued cleaning the hall and was done minutes before the conference. When he approached the fireplace, all Brothers were present.

In the middle of the group was an empty seat, obviously meant for Cody. He sat down and accepted a cup of hot cider with cookies.

Brother Ben spoke first. "Cody, we just received a call from the county jail. Everyone you counseled has signed up for community help. We have never had a visit where anyone did this. We were amazed how you could relate to those teenagers! The advice you gave was excellent and everyone followed it! Troubled teens have always been our toughest barrier. You are homegrown and seem to be the only one around here that understands them. We were beginning to think that it was impossible to reach out to them, until Cody Browne got involved!"

Then a passive voice spoke out from the end of the table; it was Brother Jonathan. "I was a successful business man for most of my life. I treated my employees well and often gave them large bonuses. Still, there was something missing. One day I realized that I would be more of a person by helping, rather than earning. I gave up my wealth to join this fellowship. As far as I am concerned, my life started when I got here. What I want to be for this town, you already are. That personal touch that gives hope to our youth is what we have been trying to tackle. You did it! We could all learn from you!"

Then another voice injected from the opposite end. It was Brother Mario. "You need to understand that your past is what has made you who you are. What you have experienced and how you survived all counts at this point. It's like an apprenticeship program; you have been educated throughout life for this special work. We don't know of anyone else that can do it."

Cody was overwhelmed! All his life he had bosses, teachers, and at times family - tell him that he'd never have a future. Often, they said to him that he would never amount to anything. At times, he even believed it! He now realized that all of his experiences, all of the failures, and every time he was wrong, created its own education! His life did count and was of value to the famous East Side Brotherhood! To assist them in any fashion was beyond any success a movie star could have; it would be the greatest honor anyone could achieve! The smile on Cody's face showed glory!

Then the Chairman stood up and said, "Follow me." Cody was led to the back room where the sleeping quarters were. He was escorted down a narrow hallway where Brother Ben opened a door.

They entered a small room that had bare necessities. There was a bed, table with two chairs, matching dresser, and night stand with a lamp. Above the bed was a beautiful picture of a sunrise over a snow covered mountain range. The room had a window with a dynamic view of the edge of town and the mountains that barricaded it. It was a tranquil setting for a great life. Brother Ben calmly said to Cody, "To some of us, this is everything!"

Then in a warm tone the Brother asked Cody if he would join the Brotherhood and take up permanent residency. Cody's mouth dropped open in shock; he couldn't speak! He was being asked to join the highest position in South Fork! He would never again have to look for a job or be homeless! Most of all, he now believed in life! He shook in disbelief and looking at Brother Ben said, "Yes, I want to join the Brotherhood!"

The Head Brother looked at the young recruit and said "Welcome aboard, Brother Cody!" A handshake with a hug followed.

The two went back to the hall where the others were patiently awaiting the verdict. With authority, Brother Ben announced, "I'd like to introduce you to Brother Cody!" The men stood up and cheered their newest member. Handshakes were given and hugs followed! Cody had arrived! Then, Cody held hands with the brothers on either side of him, forming a circle. Soon, all were holding hands. A confirmation of Cody's dedication was further exposed as he led the congregation in the Lord's Prayer. The room was united with the Brotherhood being complete.

A midnight meeting soon followed. Thanksgiving was less than two weeks away, and there would be many families to feed. The traditional Thanksgiving parade always started with the Brotherhood leading the procession. They handed out candy and fliers, telling all of the holiday dinner to be served.

This was Cody's golden moment! Every year, he watched the parade with his mother and sister. How surprised they would be seeing him as a member of the East Side Brotherhood! He would lay low from his old home life and slowly move his personal items to his new residence. He wanted this to be a well guarded secret. He kept in contact with his family and reported that he did find work. He told them that he was very busy and would meet them at the Thanksgiving Parade.

The brisk November winds blew down the icy main street of SouthFork as a crowd began to settle on its frozen sidewalks. The concerned sister accompanied by her husband and mother placed four chairs to view the up-coming event. As the final hour approached, it was obvious that Cody was nowhere to be seen. The fact that the family hadn't seen him in two weeks could only leave them wondering where he actually was or if something happened. In sadness, Jannet Browne placed a wool blanket on the vacant chair meant for her son.

The Southfork High School Marching Band began to rumble patriotic tunes as the brass instruments made the crowded streets come alive.

Then the pride of Southfork came: the East Side Brotherhood! Within a moment, Susan spotted a tall, handsome man that could only be her brother! She cried with joy seeing her once-troubled sibling passing out candy as a Brotherhood member! With excitement, she nudged her mother to direct her attention.

Pointing at the front of the parade, the daughter said, "Look, it's Cody!"

Jannet looked and had the surprise of her life! Her son was now a member of a famous organization that few were allowed to join. He had color to his skin, was well groomed, and his long hair was cut shorter. He was lean, healthy looking, and wore nice clothing. But most of all, he was happy! The neighbors sitting around the Browne family recognized him and immediately approached Jannet to congratulate her! She was never so proud in all her life!

The newest addition to the Brotherhood saw his mom and cried out, "Hey mom, come down to the fellowship hall after the parade; it's my turn to serve you Thanksgiving dinner!"

The crowd laughed as Jannet yelled back, "We'll be there, son!"

The challenged mother could only thank God. She prayed for her son every night and begged for God's grace to give him direction. Her prayers were finally answered on that Thanksgiving Day. Her son was not a misfit living off of family anymore. He was no longer the guy that never lasted long on a job and owed too many. He was now prominent within the town he grew up in and part of the driving force that it was known for. It took many trials and mistakes to learn what he was meant to be in life, but he found his way.

On that cold, fall morning, Cody Browne became a man and joined society. He was now an East Side Brother, serving the town that always took care of him.

# THE DISFIGURED MAN

THE PANDEMONIUM OF LAUGHTER bounced off walls as Paul Schmiling told another story. Red faces dropped fruit, sandwiches, and bags of chips as his side-splitting humor overwhelmed the crew. This lenient supervisor was loved by everyone and always the center of attention. Paul was also quick to imitate fellow workers, receiving more laughs. He was most famous for his impersonation of "Thomas Darling," the disfigured man that cleaned up after their breaks. It took great effort for this state issued handicap to perform his janitorial work, and Paul loved it! He even nicked-named him "Smiley" to illustrate the poor dental work he had. Paul would make light of the way he would grit his teeth with determination – to walk forward and perform his job.

It was now several minutes past the hour as the workers hastily finished their lunch. In unison, they stood up as the plastic chairs fell backwards on the floor. The room was a sty. Orange peels, plastic sandwich bags, pop cans that missed their mark, and cookie crumbs littered the once sanitized break room. The shipping department now exits the pigpen in a single-file line. Quiet now reigned in this unorthodox "no-mans-land."

Outside the break room, a frail, hunched-back figure struggles pushing a cart. Squeaky wheels signal the passing of cleaning supplies as the rambunctious workforce marches by. The considerate elder always guides his cart against the far wall, to allow extra room for others. Nobody acknowledges him.

The cleaning man continues to hobble down the hallway to his next station. Finally, he arrives at the recently occupied break room and enters. He surveys the insulting chore that awaits him and begins the monotonous task. This daily routine had to be exercised three times a day. Bathrooms, changing rooms, and the parking lot were all the victims of this great injustice.

Thomas Darling, however, never complained about this abuse. He was grateful to have a job and expressed this by working diligently, despite his handicap. He was obviously taken advantage of and never appreciated. This martyr was also greatly misunderstood.

He was well aware of his surroundings, including the ridicule that was directed at him. He purposely made noise to alert the workers of his coming presence, in case he was the topic of conversation. He even had the practice of turning around in a slow- methodical motion, allowing others not to get caught staring at him. This sensitive being was openly viewed as an invalid who was forced in by the state.

One morning, Thomas approached a room that was monopolized by Paul Schmilling's monologue. The room stifled when the disabled man entered. With his quick wit, Paul asked Thomas, "What planet do you come from anyway?" Hysterics followed as Paul controlled the audience.

With a simple smile, the Purple Heart veteran could only reply, "I wish you knew."

Thomas Darling was a disabled Vietnam veteran that survived burns over much of his body. The many plastic surgeries helped mold his deformed body to restricted use. The former college All-American applied his ability to serve his country as a soldier. He never lost his savvy and refused to become a detriment to society. Long waits at bus stops, transfers, and a physically challenging job dominated the life of this self-sufficient patriot.

There was a power that drove Thomas: his faith in God. He always felt blessed and was taught by his mother that everyone was given enough to serve their Creator. She would remind him that God only gave them assignments that they were capable of doing and promised that they would always have the tools to carry them out.

Thomas once weakened and considered suicide. His burns denied him the ability to father children and his grotesque features hampered his mobility and drew stares. He once asked a fellow volunteer from the food bank to meet him for a dinner date. He watched how uncomfortable she was facing his gruesome appearance. She apologized for the rejection and left. He felt awful, making her uncomfortable, and never forgave himself for putting her in that predicament. He continued life knowing that he was to serve God, and those actions would represent his beauty. The burn patient would never hide his scars in shame. He often visited local hospitals using himself as an example for fellow victims – to provide support and encouragement. He even posed as a monster in local charity Halloween haunted houses, passing out candy to children. He continued to volunteer at local food banks and attended church services when possible.

Friday was a sacred day for Thomas. It was his mother's birthday, and he would visit her grave site after work to deliver flowers and pray. She was there when he woke up in the burn ward back home. Her smile gave him the will to live. His mother would often say, "You're still my Thomas!"

Paul Schmilling started his Friday morning being summoned by the plant manager. He was told that a three-month project had just been completed. A prototype burner was installed with a revolutionary refractory. This fuel efficient technology would double production, using only half the natural gas. This investment would pay for itself within five years. The corporate heads were flying into town that day to see the inaugural start up. The significance of this visit would decide the direction of the plant. This construction site had many months worth of garbage that needed to be cleaned up at once! Paul was told to make sure that the mill was presentable for this tour. Thomas would be assigned to do this monumental task, alone.

Paul Schmilling relayed the orders to Thomas. He emphasized the importance of this visit by saying, "Remember, this isn't a circus. You are only here to clean the area and stay out of sight!" The former army commander shook his head in understanding as he pushed his cart towards the mill.

When Thomas arrived at the mill, he was faced by the makeshift dump. The entire area was littered by the many wooden crates that held new equipment. Scaffolding was still erected with candy wrappers and lunch bags thrown about. Welding hoses spewed across the floor, still connected to their tanks. Gallons of oil, saturated rags, paper towels, and marked where gearboxes were replaced. The torched remains of internal parts along with greasy coveralls lay randomly throughout the room.

Thomas was provided little to work with: a pallet of floor-dry, an empty trash bin, a shovel, and a broom. With time being a factor, he aggressively used the shovel to clear a path leading to the crucible. He quickly spread oil absorbent on the slick floor and continued to widen the path he created. The dedicated janitor picked up waste and placed it in the garbage bin, as he steadily cleared the filthy environment.

Thomas was conscious about the visitors arriving at any moment and worked through breaks to accomplish as much as he could. He noticed a passing forklift and motioned the driver to push the industrial size garbage bin into an abandoned supply room adjacent to the mill. This allowed him to consolidate the mess and hide it from view. His work ethic prevailed as he finished sweeping the concrete floor and lowered the ceiling bay door that would conceal the supply room. The battle of time was won, and the mill now upheld the company standard.

Like clockwork, just as the bay door closed, the tour arrived. The parade of three piece suits, company issued hard hats, and smiles of anticipation graced the caravan. The mills only entrance was a large bay door that faced the property line. This part of the plant resembled a state park. It was built on the edge of a river that allowed barges to supply raw materials. It was well manicured and surrounded by lavish green rolling hills with picnic tables.

As the management team approached their destination, the mammoth metal barrier, enclosing the renovated foundry, began to roll upward. Inside was Mill Superintendent, Dave McKnight. He was wearing a clean pair of coveralls and displayed a smile of pride. He motioned for everyone to enter and began the formality of introducing himself and shaking hands. Once the last visitor entered the confines, the bay door slowly lowered to allow privacy.

The weary custodian wandered back towards his locker to have his first meal of the day. At that moment, the ground shook with a loud rumble. Thomas looked toward the mill and saw that its metal door was concave with fire leaping through gaps created by the explosion. Within seconds, the factory emptied and crowded in front of the burning structure. The neighboring plants on the property line, and across the river, scrambled to view the disturbance.

Thomas knew from his military experience that there was a chance to save lives. Without hesitation, he saw a parked forklift and climbed in it. He then started the machine and sped to the inferno. Lowering the forks, he was able to slide them under the dented metal and tried to pry open the most damaged corner. This was where the flames reached out, serving as a beacon for the destruction inside. As the disabled custodian fought the massive door, the intense flames increased, engulfing the cast iron vehicle. The determined veteran continued to struggle with the stubborn barrier, gradually ripping a doorway-sized opening for the captives inside.

Like a herd of gazelles, the prisoners ran through the opening and rolled onto the wet grassy lawn. The crowd roared in triumph as the would-be victims escaped the jaws of death. Steam rose from partially burned clothing as everyone joined in to pat out the flames. Fire trucks and aid cars with medics arrived, quickly administering treatment. All were saved, with only a few minor injuries!

The ultimate achievement had been shared: the saving of human life! A celebration began as everyone hugged one another in gratification. Tears of relief accompanied laughter as the jubilation escalated into a frenzy. All watched as the survivors stared at one another, realizing that they would see their families that night!

The focus then turned to the gas-fed raging fire. There was a peculiar feeling as the devastated mill continued to burn. Then it dawned on everyone; the real hero was nowhere to be found! The forklift used to free the visitors was also vanished. Life momentarily stopped with the realization that Thomas was forgotten and left inside!

The valiant lift driver directed his undivided attention to free the party. He concentrated on using the mechanical jack to manipulate the flaming barrier. The small iron machine would pivot as it fought the greater mass. Thomas created an advantage by utilizing maximum power with the vintage service vehicle. He would floor-board its accelerator petal- to generate more lifting power as he got further underneath the melting wall. Finally, the weakened metal door tore open, allowing freedom for those inside. The momentum of this mobile jack caused it to roll into the blaze. The top half of the door fell to the ground when the lift passed under it, but not until all were able to escape, all but Thomas. The tonnage of crumpled metal now served as a blockade, containing the raging fire.

The disabled soldier followed his survival instincts. Like an alley cat, he found a nook by rolling under the bent iron door that enclosed the garbage bin he filled earlier. The evil hissing of pressurized natural gas could be heard, unmercifully feeding the out-of-control fire. The harbored man was now isolated from the fire...for awhile. The wicked flames were expanding their territory and started to advance through the room's only opening. The exhausted commando began to push the mighty steel bin to shield him from the penetrating heat. The greasy floor allowed the container to slide as he positioned it firmly against the wall, momentarily barricading him from the blaze. Upon contact, the flames walked up the back of the solvent-laden metal and enveloped its flammable contents. The enriched flames roared upward to the low ceiling, curling upon contact. Years of neglect permitted the discolored walls to feed the hungry fire. It spread like a manufactured log burning. The lively flames covered the rectangle ceiling and continued to crawl down the walls.

Thomas realized that he was trapped and out of options. It then occurred to him that he was already severely burned from the chain of events that led him to this cremation. He knew that his past nerve-severing wounds removed a lot of feeling, and that his adrenalin disguised today's injuries. The disabled state worker was further blessed by submitting to "shock:" nature's anesthesia. He inspected his hands and saw that they were burned beyond recovery. His nylon jacket had melted on him with hot toxic smoke filling his lungs, all pain-free.

He knew that he was being blessed as he sat in the center of the room- accepting death. The reverent man could only laugh at the situation. There were times he didn't want to be alive but persevered each day to serve his Creator. Thomas would frequently cry from the haunted memories that came from battlefields. The many screams, cries of pain, and senseless deaths, accompanied by the stench of burning flesh, would surround the hell as he performed his duty. He secretly wanted to perish in those fields and join the many that were sacrificed there.

He wondered about those outside that were watching him burn at the altar. Which one would discover "Smiley's" mutilated body first? The craggy grin that only a skeleton could give would display his crude dental work, making identification easy. Would any have the courage to attend his services? Surely, his past would be displayed with the traditional American flag draped over the pine box. His highly decorated military jack would lay silent on top of his coffin as a lone trumpet would play "Taps." Loved ones from the many charitable organizations would be there to introduce themselves as a friend of the deceased. His glory days as a football player would bring former teammates, memorabilia, and many stories. Pictures of this once handsome athlete would adorn the chapel.

God's omnipresent entity overwhelmed Thomas as he extended his arms to be caressed. The devoted servant could now feel his mother's presence as he drew nearer to the eternal reunion. Like the famous monk in Saigon, he was oblivious to the horror of being burned alive. The mortal body began to lean as remaining life continued to evaporate. The maimed soldier was completing his journey. His mission was fulfilled, having earned every merit badge life offered.

In glory, he would leave this world with the valor only known to heroes. God's loving grace would permit the disfigured man to die this day with the soul of Thomas Robert Darling's granted passage.

# Your Quiet Neighborhood

# THE THREE BERRY CAPER

A LARGE GATHERING assembled at the town square to commemorate an important milestone. This was the one-hundred and fifty year anniversary of Pioneer Valley, with a celebration underway! A parade led by the local marching band was followed by its highly decorated drill team. Floats sponsored by local businesses displayed their colors like a proud peacock. A procession of vintage cars slowly drove down the main street with the reigning beauty queen waving to the community she represented. The mayor smiled and shook hands as he passed out pamphlets. All clubs were represented with vendors selling memorabilia. The aroma of barbeque ribs, chicken, hotdogs, and hamburgers tantalized the hungry crowd. This festive occasion helped ease the tension of this divided town.

The original settlers started a feud amongst themselves that was still unresolved. The cold-war of Pioneer Valley consisted between two families: "Smith" and "Cromwell." It all started when one family named a road after themselves. The other reciprocated in defense. When the railroad tracks were laid through the small town, the community was then divided. The tracks now served as a boundary between the self-named streets and their families. Like a "Dr. Seuss " story, "control" was the issue with absurd rumors stirring the pot. This town was not without merit though. It was famous for its "Three Berry Preserve," a unique blend – of three unique berries- that always won every blue ribbon at county fairs.

Many theorized on what made these berries different: Some say that the mild climate in the foothills benefited from the pure mountain air. Others claim that the soil was perfected for the berries, since they were the only crop ever grown there. Folklore credited the historical town for keeping the recipe a secret, to honor their heritage. The three berry preserve was often imitated, but the code was never cracked! Once a product of "Pioneer Valley Three Berry Preserves" was delivered to a store, they sold out fast! Like the famous "Copper River Salmon," this was a seasonal goldmine that allowed this town of independent farmers to survive.

The covet berries were not easy to get. The blackberries, which represented one-third of this Ozark recipe, could be found off of Berry Street, where the train depot was. Acres of bushes graced the station that was heart of this quaint town. These bushes were respected and shared by the community for the berry season. Then came the hard part: the much needed raspberries were located on the East side  of town with the required blueberries on the West side of town. Regardless of having one-third of the sacred berries on family property, one would have to share the international waters of the train depot and then have political asylum to gain access to their rivals' bushes. The last third of this recipe was always a challenge, whether you were a "Smith," or a "Cromwell."

Derek Smith meticulously assembled his wooden fruit stand off of Smith Street as the noon train slowly traveled through town. Once the train passed, the obstructed view of Cromwell Street was now exposed with Albert Cromwell constructing his stand. The two classmates were bonded by wearing their high school football jerseys. The teammates smiled and waved to one another as the berry season approached.

The interaction between locals was not always as friendly. Often, the smug arrogance of one family member would deny hospitality to an opposing family member. Sometimes, the town's lone barbershop would abruptly change the topic of conversation- if the wrong person entered. It was common to see someone leave an establishment, to avoid a neighbor from "the wrong side of the tracks."

There was a common ground of justice in Pioneer Valley: the retirement home on Berry Street. This old structure housed the wise seniors that once played in that very town. Every family had a relative in this "old-folks home." When anyone had a problem, their last resort would be to make a pilgrimage to this residence and seek advice.

That's what Derek Smith did. His grandfather, Harry, suggested that he wear his high school football jersey so that cross-town students could see that they had something in common. It worked like a charm! Every berry season he would give a five pound basket of raspberries to his teammate across the street and receive an equal amount of Cromwell blueberries in return. Business was good! When his cousin, Timothy, anxiously waited for the annual fishing derby, he became concerned on how to secure the best spot at the fishing hole- every year. Derek advised him to visit "Grandpa Harry" and discuss the problem with him.

Timothy Smith got up early that Saturday and took the short walk to Berry Street, to visit his grandfather. The frisky old man was elated to receive a visit from his youngest grandson. He was even more touched to discover the young lad came for advice. The thoughtful child presented his grandfather with a homemade card, showing appreciation for his role in the family. He then hugged the elder and began to share his problem.

"Grandpa," addressed a somber Timothy Smith.

"Yes, Timothy," replied the caring old man.

"Do you know about the fishing tournament coming up next week?" inquired the child.

"Yes," answered the grandfather. "I helped dig that pond so boys like you could fish in it one day!"

"Really?" exclaimed Timothy.

"Really," said the soft spoken senior.

"Every year, we have a hard time getting a good spot for the fishing derby," said Timothy. "What do we do about that?"

"Share," replied the wise owl. "Why don't you show up early so that you can be there first? Then, you can purposely allow others to claim it, knowing that you could have had it first. They will notice your consideration and offer to share it out of respect. You will even make new friends!"

Timothy's face lit up with a smile as he saw the beauty of this idea! He then hugged his grandfather, giving many thanks. The enthused youth then excused himself to devise a plan. The proud grandpa leaned back with a smile, as he remembered what it was like to be young!

Jessy Cromwell approached his older brother, Albert, to ask a question.

"Al, did you ever fish in the fishing derby?" asked Jessy.

"Sure I did," responded the brother. "Every kid in town enters that contest until they're too old."

"Did you and your friends ever have a problem trying to get a good spot to fish?" asked the bewildered little brother.

"Not at first," replied Albert. "When I was your age, that pond had two docks. When we got older, the city had to remove one; I never knew why."

"Every year it gets crowded, and sometimes we arrive too late to get our favorite spot," said Jessy. "What can we do about this?"

Albert gave a long pause and reflected on a past experience. "I once had a similar problem. I didn't know how to get raspberries to make three berry preserves for my fruit stand. I finally addressed this predicament to Papa Cromwell, and he gave me a solution!"

"What did he say?" asked an intrigued Jessy.

"Papa told me that everyone always has something that someone else needs," explained the big brother. "He told me to share my berries with someone who needed them and could share what I needed. My friend, Derek, needed some of my berries, and I needed some of his. We both realized that we were classmates and played football together. That made him a friend the whole time, and we now supply each other during the berry season! You need to visit Papa Cromwell and get his advice!"

"When can we visit him?" asked the excited boy.

"How about after dinner?" suggested Albert. "If your homework is done, we will walk to where he lives and ask him!"

Jessy smiled and quickly ran to his room to finish his school work.

The time was now six o'clock with one hour left for visitation. The brothers walked the five minute journey to Berry Street, to visit their wise grandfather. Such visits were always special, as the offspring would bring mother's homemade cookies as a gift.

Clarence Cromwell was pleasantly surprised to see his two favorite grandchildren pay a much welcomed visit. "Papa" just finished his own dinner and enjoyed the chocolate chip cookies his daughter made.

The big man hugged the boys with emotion. He then asked, "What did I do to deserve seeing you two today?"

"Albert spoke first, "Papa, we need to get your opinion about something."

"Why sure," replied the honored senior.

Jessy then asked, "Papa, do you know about the fishing derby coming up?"

"Yes," exclaimed the elder, "that event has been a part of this town for over fifty years!"

"Did you ever catch fish there?" asked the younger grandson.

"No," replied Papa Cromwell, "that pond was only meant for children. But, I have taken your mother there many times, and she has caught lots of fish!"

"My friends' and I can't always get our spot at the derby," explained Jessy. "The other boys usually get there before we do and take it." Then with a concerned look on his face, he asked his mentor, "What can we do?"

The crafty old man thought for awhile, and then displayed a huge grin as he thought up a remedy. "I know," he proclaimed with enthusiasm. "Your mother's cookies will get you that spot," said the elated elder as he displayed a chocolate chip delight and ate it. "Your mom will bake more so that you can share them with the boys that have the spot. They will love them, just as I do! They will know that you are a friend and allow you to fish with them!

Jessy grinned at his brother, acknowledging his sound advice. After a brief visit, they ran home to coordinate this peace offering with their mother.

The following Saturday was the much anticipated fishing derby. Timothy had a slumber party at his parent's house, with his fishing buddies attending. Derek would chaperone the anglers to the derby after their sunrise breakfast. Their earlier than normal departure had, once again, granted them their favorite fishing spot. However, they had agreed to leave it vacant to show diplomacy to their competitors.

Moments later, Jessy's group arrived- running to the unclaimed territory. As they approached the dock, Timothy's party was spotted, obviously allowing them to claim the place of choice. Both knew that the first arrivals showed courtesy, not to hoard the lone dock. They also brought cookies as a barter to share that very location. Time passed as the "ball was in their court." Timothy's group waited for the consideration to be reciprocated. The boys on the dock huddled in conference. Finally, one left the pack and walked toward the others.

A hand was extended as the messenger introduced himself. He pointed out that there was enough room for both parties and invited them to join. The boys smiled in appreciation and accepted the invitation! Timothy had brought a large thermos of hot chocolate with extra paper cups. His friends introduced one another as the hot drink was shared. Chocolate chip cookies from Jessy's household were handed out, as the boys watched fish jump. The derby was to start in an hour, with the groups uniting and starting a new tradition!

The fishing derby was a success, with all the boys receiving prizes for the largest fish caught! Jessy and Timothy would secretly have their mothers' prepare a trout dinner for their wonderful grandfathers, as a gift for teaching them a valuable lesson in life.

The berry season was to start in a few days. This was the time of year where all members of the community had to "bury the hatchet." It was crucial for each side of the tracks to have a part in the other: "You can only make hay when the sun is shining." The berry harvest was projected to be the highest yield in years, with the good will of gift-giving underway!

The school kids were the first wave of battle. They were the ponds that would take small plastic bags of home-grown berries to school and trade them with anyone that didn't share their last name. Like a courtship, one "adult" member of a household would contact the family whose child thoughtfully gave their child a sample of the precious fruit- to give thanks. Eventually, visits were arranged where larger quantities of the homegrown produce would be exchanged as "gifts."

The competition of giving provided the necessary "third" to produce their own three-berry preserves. Local restaurants benefited from these acts of diplomacy, and church attendance would reach its yearly high. This modern day rendition of Easter egg hunting and Halloween trick-or-treat seemed to be a ritual all within itself. But it did supply the demand!
The senior women of the valley seemed to have the best approach. Several months before berry harvest, a well-coordinated quilting party would meet once a week. The weak spot on the opposite side of the

103

tracks would be graced with a hand-made quilt that would match the victims wallpaper. Berries were also given to "set the stage." Knitted sweaters, cords of wood, rides to town, and a multitude of compliments were all used as arsenal. The town was in a friendly battle to get full use out of every last berry.

Orders as far away as Europe, Asia, and Denmark patiently waited for the seasonal jams, jellies, syrups, and pies that only came from this part of the world! This limited supply of three-berry preserves came from the happy American town of "Pioneer Valley!"

Sunday evening was the eve of harvest, the calm before the storm. Derek Smith had an early dinner and walked through the quiet town to visit his grandfather. As he approached his quarters, intense laughter could be heard coming from the room. He slowly pushed the door that was partially opened. He was amused to find his grandfather in hysterics with Clarence Cromwell. They were laughing at the news on television, showing the local merchants preparing for the upcoming berry season.

"What's so funny?" asked the puzzled teenager.

"Well, we have to tell somebody," laughed Harry Smith.

"Can we trust you with a secret?" bellowed out Papa Cromwell.

A curious Derek slowly responded with caution, "What is it?"

"What do you know about this town's history?" asked his grandfather.

Derek paused and said, "I know that we are one of the oldest towns in the country."

"Anything else?" asked Mr. Cromwell as he fought back the laughter.

"You mean the feud?" asked the somber young man.

"Yes," cried out the family elder.

"What's so special about this time of year?" asked Clarence.

"The berry harvest," answered Derek.

"What makes it so challenging?" asked Harry Smith.

"We have to respect everyone in order to make our three-berry preserves," answered the inquisitive visitor.

Then both men yelled, "That's right" and doubled up laughing for the next minute.

Derek looked with astonishment and asked, "What's wrong with that?"

The men yelled back, "Nothing! It should always be that way!" Their violent laughter continued for several more minutes.

Derek couldn't understand their comments and asked, "Why?"

"Derek, do you know what we did for a living before we retired?" asked his grandfather.

"I only know that you both worked for the city," he replied. We were like you; we didn't like the feud either. We decided to get involved with city legislature and planning. We did an "inside job" to fight this problem. Do you know why the berry bushes are spread apart within this town?

A confused Derek answered, "We were taught in local history that the berries would not survive if they were planted too close together. They each attracted different insects that would kill the other two species. They had to be far apart in order for all three to grow.

"Son," remarked his senior father figure, "that was a wives tale. We conjured up that rumor to separate them on opposite sides of this town.

"Why?" asked the confused high school student.

Harry Smith continued, "We initially had all the berry bushes concentrated on Berry Street, the same area that now only has blackberries. When the feud started to escalate, the berries were becoming the first casualty. There was no respect for one another, and the natural resource of this town was being hoarded by neighbors, working against each other. We had to intervene- to allow those berries to grow. We conjured up that story as a ploy to force this town to cooperate for survival.

Derek smiled as he understood the logic. He then asked if there were any more secrets.

The men looked at each other to gain approval; then Clarence said, "There are a few more. That fishing hole that holds the derbies used to have two docks.

We altered our weight limit on fishing docks so that only one could legally be there. I think you know why. At one time, this town actually had two high schools. We modified the budget so that only one could exist here. We looked at the mascots of the former schools, the "Panthers" and the "Tigers." We blended the logo to "Wildcats." The red colors of one school and blue of the other were mixed to give us the purple and white we now have."

Grandfather Smith yelled out, "And every time a Cromwell scored a touchdown, there was a Smith blocking for him! We have had our share of State Championships since the schools merged!"

The visit was momentarily interrupted by a knock at the door. Derek opened it and was surprised to see Albert Cromwell's aunt. "I thought that I saw you coming in here," she said in a polite tone. "My sewing club made this nice blazer. We think that it would look beautiful with that blouse your mother wears to church. And, before I forget, here are some blueberries from our garden; we think your family will like them!"

"Thank you, Mrs. Cromwell." said Derek. "My mother will appreciate this very much! I will give this to her tonight and have her call you."

"Oh, I would love to hear from her," exclaimed Nora Cromwell. "Bye!" The sweet neighbor from the opposite side of the tracks left the room with a smile on her face.

Derek was dumbfounded now that he knew the towns "real" history. He stared at the floor absorbing the shock; then he looked at the lifelong friends, and smiled.

The wise old men looked at the young man holding the gifts and nodded in approval.

Derek said his good-byes and walked home, consumed by what he had just learned. The town he lived in seemed to be one – big "dis-functional family," and it was! Like any wedding or holiday celebration, many incorporate a facade to endure what was necessary. He couldn't understand why the town couldn't accept everyone simply the way they were, like he and his friend Albert did. Then, he realized that they bonded- based on the cleverness of their grandfathers. The enlightened youth could only shake his head laughing at everyone, including himself.

# SMALL TOWN 101

THE LANGLY COMMUNITY CHURCH paused in silence to collect much needed tithes. The congregation was struggling through hard times as weekly donations continued to fall.

Glenn Royals reached into his deep pockets and produced another sizable check. Pastor Mighten smiled in gratitude as the town's wealthiest man continued to support the church. His compassion seemed to be a curse as neighbors became dependent on him. Glenn was now expected to help those who asked. His image changed from being a charitable man to a despised landlord.

The church service came to an end as everyone stood. The pews closest to the altar emptied first. The patrons quietly left the wooden structure adorned with stained glass. Pastor Mighten was the first to exit and greeted his parishioners in the main lobby. He always approached Glenn Royals with an extended hand.

"We certainly appreciate what you do for us!" proclaimed Pastor Mighten.

"It's my pleasure to serve the Lord!" replied Glenn. The warm handshake escalated to a hug, with the two men revealing God's grace. There were more people to visit as Glenn left the church and crossed the street. He mingled with familiar faces he would see throughout the week. He continued to walk towards the town's lone gas station and entered. This was just one of his many businesses.

"Good morning, Mr. Royals!" exclaimed the clerk.

"Mr. Royals is my father!" stated the proprietor. "My name is Glenn!" The warm man smiled at the teenager and inquired, "How is your day, Teresa?"

The young woman blushed. "Fine, Glenn!"

"How about enjoying this fine morning and take a few hours off, with pay?" suggested Glenn. "I'll run the store for a while. You can be back here by noon."

"Thank you, Mr. Royals; I mean, Glenn!" The employee left.

The image of this humanitarian continued to decompose. Bill Fossell entered the establishment and was stunned to see Glenn Royals behind the counter. It was obvious that Bill avoided Glenn.

"I don't have the money yet," said Bill

"That's okay," said Glenn. "You can charge as much as you want."

Bill had pride and looked up at Glenn. "You must love the feeling of being such a powerful man. You actually run this town."

"I don't have any power; I have been blessed with the good fortune of being able to run my business," replied Glenn.

"You think God is the reason why you have so much?" Bill retorted. "The meek are the ones who will inherit the earth."

Glenn didn't know what to say. He was being addressed by a neighbor who had apparently turned on him. He lent money to Bill and allowed him to charge anything in his store. He was also his landlord and allowed several months' worth of rent to be excused. He never asked to be paid back. Glenn helped others and never used success as leverage. He only had one dream, and that was to live in a small town where everyone cared for one another.

"Why don't you stay here with your kingdom!" exclaimed Bill. He left without getting any supplies. That bothered Glenn knowing that Bill was going through hard times. What made matters worse was that he was now being denied helping someone.

The tempo changed within seconds as Phil Swanson entered the station. Phil was Glenn's closest friend in town. "Good morning, handsome!" greeted Phil.

"Good morning to you!" replied Glenn.

"That was quite a sermon Pastor gave today," remarked Phil.

"I loved it!" said Glenn.

The bantering volleyed back and forth for several minutes.

"Do you work all day?" asked Phil.

"I hope not," laughed Glenn. "My helper should be back before noon."

"We are having a barbeque this afternoon," said Phil. "Why don't you drop by?"

"Ya got a date!" said a smiling Glenn Royals. "Should I bring anything?"

"No, just yourself," replied Phil.

Glenn's spirits were raised by this visit. He looked forward to an afternoon in a friend's back yard.

Phil shook Glenn's hand and said, "I have to get a haircut now; see you later!" He left for the barber shop.

Teresa returned to her job. Glenn enjoyed a brief visit with the young woman and left for the barbeque.

The quaint town was convenient for pedestrians, with everything being within walking distance. Glenn left his enterprise and walked by the barber shop that led to Phil's home. He passed "Sam's Barber Shop" and saw the retirees who gathered there. Glenn stuck his head in the door.

"Hello, everyone!" said Glenn.

"Hi, Glenn," answered the group.

The visit proved joyous as everyone teased and laughed at one another. A peculiar event would then take place. Phil asked Glenn if he could borrow one hundred dollars. Glenn immediately opened his wallet without question. The room respected Phil's dignity and came to a silence. Glenn handed Phil a one hundred dollar bill.

"You can take your time paying it back," said Glenn.

Phil accepted the money. "Thanks, Glenn."

Glenn respected his friend by changing the subject. "Hey!" he said, pointing at the retired police chief. "You have to be nice to me, I'm still on parole!" Laughter erupted as Glenn waved good-bye and left.

The engagement at Phil's home would start in an hour. This gave Glenn ample time to go home and prepare for the afternoon. His travels would take him by his apartment complex.

He inspected the beauty of his freshly painted building. The lawn was well manicured with colorful flowers and bushes enhancing the courtyard. It was a wonderful place to live. The satisfaction of taking care of his tenants was soon interrupted, however. Someone was calling out his name.

"Mr. Royals!" called out a tenant. It was Mrs. Woodrow, and she seemed to be in a panic.

"What is it, Megan?" asked Glenn.

113

The elder had tears in her eyes as she addressed her landlord. "I hate to do this to you again, but we will be late for rent this month." She pleaded with Glenn for mercy.

The compassionate man smiled at Megan and said, "Is that all it is?" He then gave her a warm hug. "Everybody is late on occasion; don't worry about it."

The grateful woman looked at Glenn and said, "Thank you; you're such a good man!"

Glenn smiled and said, "Everything is alright, Megan. Now stop that crying!" Mrs. Woodrow broke into relief and chuckled. The entrepreneur continued to walk home. Half of his tenants were delinquent on their rent, affecting his ability to pay the mortgage. His engagement with Phil would take his mind off this anxiety.

Glenn arrived home pondering on the financial woes his acquaintances gave him. The bachelor changed from his church clothes and left for the barbeque.

He smelled charcoal burning as he approached the house. The open gate leading to the backyard was obviously a signal for Glenn. He walked on the staggered stepping stones that were placed on the lawn. He was seen by the Swanson family as he passed through the gate.

"There's the man of the hour!" exclaimed Phil as he walked up to Glenn. Phil's wife, Sandy, and his sons, John and Mark, greeted their guest. The two friends shook hands as Phil pointed at a cooler full of beverages. Glenn helped himself to a beer. He would be the only visitor.

Phil cheered his neighbor as they tapped their beers together. "How do you like your steak cooked?" asked the host.

"Medium rare," replied Glenn.

"I'll prepare the food," said the charming wife.

The men left the patio and walked up the elevated deck. It was now a tranquil moment as they gazed over the secluded backyard. It was surrounded by a rustic wooden fence. Antique wine barrels with rusted metal bands held gorgeous flowers. They were strategically placed throughout the yard. A traditional shed occupied a corner of the lot  and matched the fence and barrels. Farming tools from last century were displayed on its exterior.

The centerpiece was a decayed tow truck of yesterday. It was enshrined on a mound that was accompanied with small maple trees and large rocks. Baskets with flowers hung from the obsolete vehicle as extra wine barrels displayed more plants. This was a masterpiece.

Glenn Royals savored the small paradise and remarked, "You have Heaven on Earth right here!"

Phil digested the compliment and said, "That's all we want."

The picnic table was set. Potato salad, steaming cobs of corn, fruit, and the best barbequed steaks in town awaited. "Time to eat!" announced Sandy.

Everyone gathered at the table and sat down. Phil led grace, and the feast began! Glenn tasted his food saying, "What a great meal!" A conversation spawned, ranging in topics. Humorous stories generated laughter, with everyone contributing. Finally, Glenn asked a question.

"Phil, there's something I have always been meaning to ask you," he said.

"What is it?" asked Phil.

"I don't understand the jokes about you being a 'descendant'," said Glenn.

Phil sat back in his chair, trying to control his laughter. He was caught off guard with his mouth full of food. The family turned quiet as they stared at one another. The father recovered and said, "That all started with our last name." Glenn was intrigued.

"The neighboring town's main street is called 'Swanson,' just like our last name. The family the street is named after are essentially the 'Rockefellers' of this county. Because of that coincidence, my family was accused of being rich. There were always people who wanted to borrow money or have us invest with them. Charities solicited us for substantial donations constantly. It eventually got to be too much, and we let everyone know that we are not the rich Swansons of that town. I still get teased about the name, however. It's a curse to be rich in a small town."

That explanation hit home with Glenn. *He* was the 'Rockefeller' of that town. It definitely wasn't easy.

The barbeque made Sunday afternoon complete. Homemade strawberry shortcake, coffee, and a brilliant sunset finished the day. Glenn expressed his appreciation to the family and left for home.

He couldn't sleep that night. He kept thinking about what Phil said: "It's a curse to be rich in a small town."

Monday was a few hours away. The business man would get up early and have breakfast at his diner. His morning routine consisted of walking through the community and randomly inspecting his interests. The latter half of the day would be focused on accounting and paying bills. If all went smooth, he would visit his tavern. Like a politician, Glenn would shake hands and buy a round of drinks. However, the day turned out bad and was full of complications.

His diner was being sued by a local resident claiming food poisoning. What made matters worse, it was a long-time customer who he often ate with and bought meals for. "Why didn't he just call me and tell me of this problem?" Glenn asked himself. He took the legal documents and called the firm representing the petitioner.

His luck continued when he visited his gas station. Someone on the night shift had embezzled money. This hurt Glenn. Whoever it was, they had received many bonuses and gift cards over the years. They knew that their boss always had an open door policy. This crime wasn't necessary, but Glenn wouldn't file a police report. He would allow the employee time to confess. He was even willing to give that person a second chance.

Glenn was frustrated beyond hope. He felt a visit at his tavern would give him the comfort of friends. His intention was to open up his wallet and buy several rounds for everyone, including lunch. However, Glenn would strike-out for a third time. He marched to his place of refuge and entered the front door. But before he approached the bar, he heard his name mentioned.

It was coming from a booth isolated in the corner.

"That Royals must like being a slave master!" said a drunken customer. Bill recognized the voice; it was Gary Lighten.

"He owns me, too!" said another. It was the unmistakable voice of Pat Wales; both were tenants and employees who owed him money on both fronts.

"I have to see that man to earn a living, then I have to pay him to live!" said Gary.

"I remember when he was new to this town; everyone thought that he was such a humble guy," said Pat.

The drinking buddies were enjoying beer and running up sizable tabs. Furthermore, they never thanked him for his generosity. Like most people in the community, Glenn never received a Christmas card from them, either. The lone man certainly gave to this community, especially during the holidays.

He had at least one friend in town: Phil Swanson. He would drop by Phil's house that evening for emotional support. Glenn went home to recover, refusing to answer any phone calls. At nightfall, he left his house to knock on his friend's door.

Glenn walked to Phil's porch and knocked on the door. It opened in seconds. Phil was pleasantly surprised to see Glenn and invited him inside.

"Glenn, it's great to see you!" said Phil.

"Thanks," said Glenn. "Can we talk?"

Phil could see a worried look on Glenn's face. He motioned him to the back deck they were on the day before. "Would you like a beer?" the host asked.

"That sounds good," Glenn replied. Phil went to the kitchen and returned with two beers. They leaned on the wooden railings in silence as the sun set.
"What's troubling you?" Phil inquired.

Glenn looked off into the horizon and sipped his beer. "It's something you said yesterday that I now understand. It *is* a curse being rich in a small town." He looked at his friend and continued, "I am not actually that rich, but everyone thinks I am. It really is a curse!"

Phil smiled at Glenn with understanding. He then remembered something. "Oh, I owe you some money, follow me."

Phil led Glenn down the stairs that touched the patio. He walked towards the old tow truck. Glenn raised an eyebrow with curiosity as he watched Phil swing the crane, positioning it over a small boulder. He lowered the cable that rolled on rusted pulleys and made a loop like a hangman's noose. The cable was lowered and wrapped around the boulder.

He looked at Glenn and said, "Now here's the fun part; better cover your ears!" He leaned into the driver's compartment and started the motor! A loud, rattling purr came from the Briggs and Stratton engine. Phil used the crane to flip over the large rock. He got on his hands and knees where the rock was resting. Phil began to dig with his fingers, exposing a chain. He fastened it to the cable and raised it with the boom. A metal box broke through the dirt. The container was removed from the hole it was buried in and placed on the ground next to it. He removed the chain and opened it.

Glenn looked over Phil's shoulder and giggled at the contents. It held bundles of neatly stacked hundred dollar bills. Phil removed a bill and handed it to Glenn. "I owe you an apology for using you at the barber shop the other day. I prefer a low profile."

Glenn could only grin with the cleverness his friend displayed. He asked, "Are you really a descendent?"

Phil stood at attention and said, "Fourth generation Swanson!"

Glenn pointed at him and said, "And nobody knows!" He then covered his stomach and fell down laughing. "I have thought of doing that myself!" Glenn said between fits of laughter.

"You need to," replied his friend. "We were in your situation before we moved here. Neighbors started to hate us because they thought we should be giving more and more. Over here, everyone looks at us as struggling, just like everyone else. Nobody bothers us now."

Glenn looked at Phil and said, "I made a decision today; I am going to sell all of my businesses. If that doesn't work, I'll give them away."

Phil asked, "Do you know where you are going?"

"Yes," replied Glenn. "I am looking at property in the next town. It's several miles past the shopping center, off Swanson Road. It's secluded acreage with a fish pond. It also has a boulder on the back lot..."

Glenn was revitalized as he tapped his beer with Phil's. "Bring your fishing pole when you visit!" he said.

# THE TOWN TERROR

THE SUN SET over snow capped mountains creating a pastel light show. The North Star had already peered through the fall sky as others came into focus. Street lamps that displayed an old world charm from last century began to light up in sequence. Friday night finally arrived in the lone town of Valiant.

The population of five hundred and twelve would now enjoy the awaited weekend. Many would go to Main Street for dinner or to see a movie. This was the opportunity that Shaun Baker waited for. He was the town's self-proclaimed "bad boy," and always felt the need to prove himself.

Shaun was a product of divorce. He was raised by his grandparents and felt abandoned. His feelings of rejection were further enhanced by being one of the shortest males in the county. This awareness scarred him with a Napoleon Complex. Shaun was bottled up

122

with anger over his insecurities. He would infiltrate society by picking fights in an attempt to be noticed and respected. He was a pariah.

His bedroom showed the turning point of his life. His grandparents accepted custody of their grandson at age six. They knew that he needed direction and enrolled him in the Cub Scouts.

Shaun loved being involved with a fellowship and applied himself. He was proud to wear his uniform when he marched in local parades. The young boy also learned survival skills that could be utilized when camping with his parents, a dream that never happened. As he grew, he saw less and less of his mother and father.

The bedroom was his sanctuary. It displayed numerous merit badges that he had earned. It also had a window that showed the countryside. The darkness of a clear night was special to him. He would create imaginary friends by connecting stars together. They all had names, with some waving at him. Unlike his parents, "Twinkle," "Fairy," "Spaceman," and the others were always there - even if it was raining.

The main event would be when the midnight train would rumble through the valley. It didn't come every night and often weeks apart. His grandfather once pointed it out when they had a camp out on their property.

"Do you see that?" cried out the grandfather. "That's what we call the train of salvation! It got its name many years ago when your great grandfather was a child. It would purposely slow down at every town it passed through when it had empty flat cars. This meant that there was work down the line and any available help could hop on and get hired. Your great grandfather Donald arrived in this town riding that train. Laws have since been passed that frown on this tradition. They will still pick up workers that need to get their lives started but only late at night."

The young Shawn grinned at the powerful locomotive. Its headlamp cast light on the tracks it traveled on. The train did slow down passing through the edge of town as a figure could be seen climbing aboard a vacant flatcar. In minutes, the train gained speed and blew its whistle as it penetrated the night, traveling out of sight. Like a young boy listening to an old sea captain, Shaun yearned for the adventure.

Shaun's childhood seemed short lived. He was now twenty and rebellious. His room also had additions with court orders and fines displayed as trophies. The unemployed grandson chose the isolation of his bedroom when his grandparents were home. He was no longer their sweet grandchild and talked back to them. He was a punk refusing to grow up.

Brandie's Bar and Grill was the local hot spot. It was always full on a Friday night with friends, music, and laughter. The benches surrounding the main entrance were usually occupied with more customers. The "who's who" would be there. Shaun would select this nightspot for his battleground.

It was dinnertime and Shaun was getting ready for town. He groomed his mustache, but he wasn't Burt Reynolds. He brushed his 1970's rock 'n roll hair style but was nobody famous. He made sure he had his pocket knife and left.

His driver's license was suspended, forcing his grandparents to restrict the use of their car. The small town, however, was convenient to walk through. In minutes, Brandie's festive neon sign and Christmas lights came into view. The evening was underway with couples holding hands and friends meeting. This harmony angered Shaun; he was an outcast.

As he approached the establishment, a sensitive issue presented itself. Deloris Hedman was entering the restaurant with her boyfriend, Stan English. Deloris was Shaun's high school crush, and Stan was that popular guy he always envied. This made Shaun jealous and motivated him to confront the couple. Shaun entered the  dining area as the couple sat down. He glared at Stan and challenged him to a fight.

"What a wuss," exclaimed the overweight intruder. "I'm gonna kick some ass!"

Stan was in control and replied with class. "Shaun, we are having a great evening, and we don't need your trouble here," he replied.

The mature diplomacy further aggravated Shaun. "Are you afraid of me?" he challenged.

"No, only embarrassed for you," replied Stan. "You are always alone and create problems wherever you go. You are still a child."

Shaun instinctively threw a punch that hit Stan in the shoulder. Stan stood up and countered with a right to Shaun's jaw, dropping him. The couple left the restaurant and went to the diner across the street. The sheriff arrived and took statements. Many witnessed the event and gave reports. Shaun was handcuffed and sent to jail.

It was almost nine o'clock that night when Shaun's grandparents arrived at the police station. Bail was posted, and the three left. The ride was quiet. When they arrived home, they tried to talk to him, but he wouldn't listen. He went to his room and slammed the door shut. This was a typical Friday night for Shaun. He looked for trouble and found it. His grandparents were hurt. They didn't know what they could do for him.

He spent that night awake. In his mind, he was the victim. He felt he was treated unfairly in the community and needed to show everyone that he was somebody. Shaun was frustrated from the embarrassment he received in town. He was also cursed with being stubborn and vindictive. He would return to the scene of the crime to win a battle... or so he thought.

Saturday morning arrived with Shaun being distant from his grandparents. He would avoid the worn out lectures he had heard many times before. He was patiently waiting for the evening and his chance to redeem himself.

When nightfall arrived, Shaun left for town. The autumn chill had Shaun button up his wool coat. The determined soul began to breathe heavily in anticipation as his breath vaporized before him. He was on a mission. Main Street was now a few steps away with Brandie's down the street. The house was full; it was Saturday night!

Shaun approached the bar and grill as joyous memories were being created. A public bonfire gave warmth to the many patrons that waited for seating. Smiles with laughter filled the night air. The serenity of this congregation was in contrast to Shaun's life. He was jealous and wanted to destroy it. The perfect opportunity was spotted. Billy Fields could be seen through the dining room window.

Billy was gigantic in stature. His mountain man appearance was always clothed in coveralls with a large flannel shirt. His wavy dark hair accented his manly beard. This heavyweight always won events at county logging shows. The biggest quality of this giant was his heart. He was a God-fearing gentleman that always had a smile for everyone.. He would never hurt a fly and always tipped his hat to a lady. Shaun selected this specimen to challenge in public.

Shaun barged into the restaurant in a rage. The room silenced having seen Shaun Baker's entrance. As usual, he arrived alone and came to cause trouble. He naturally confronted Billy and challenged him to a fight.

"I'm gonna kick some ass," Shaun cried out. "Stand up and fight!"

Something different happened. The entire room groaned in disappointment over Shaun's childish behavior. At once, everyone in the dining room got up to leave. Rejection was Shaun's worst fear. In defiance, he stood in front of the entryway to prevent anyone from using the front door. The crowd refused to be around him and opened windows to crawl out. Others walked through the kitchen and found the back door.

Shaun was dumbfounded. The famous Brandie's Bar and Grill was being abandoned by every means. Everyone left the premises to get away from him. They all went different directions and called it a night. Immediately, he reversed his diplomacy by trying to apologize. The embarrassed, tough guy went out into the street trying to shake hands with the protestors. It was too little, too late. He was ignored.

In moments, the lights to Brandie's were turned off with the doors locked. The streets were now quiet with only one figure present. That lone person would have a long walk home to his grandparent's house. He began to shuffle his feet while staring at the ground...thinking.

Shaun mentally reviewed the evening. The rejection neutered him like a dog. He dug deeper into his past and remembered that at one time he did have a few friends. The evening was still early, and he could look up phone numbers and make contact.

He arrived at his grandparent's homestead. The quaint cottage sat proudly on a hill that overlooked the outskirts of town. Dirt roads and train tracks were the only neighbors. He walked the path leading to the wooden structure and entered the home. His grandparents were in the living room, watching television. It was noticeable that their grandson was preoccupied with a problem. They remained quiet as he went to his room.

Shaun was now in his bedroom and closed the door. He got his high school yearbook and began thumbing through the pages. A familiar face was eventually found. He spotted Gregg Hutch. Gregg was a sidekick that introduced cigarettes into Shaun's life. The like minded duo shared a bond by being hooligans.

Shaun looked up Gregg's phone number on the back of the annual and called. The phone rang for a few seconds; then it was answered by a woman.

"Hello," called out a soft aging voice.

"Hello, this is Shaun Baker," replied Shaun. "Is Greg there?"

There was a long pause as Mrs. Hutch recovered from the shock of Shaun's contact. "Greg is gone," she answered. "My son joined the navy and is stationed in Pensacola, Florida. We won't see him until Christmas." The mother hung up the phone.

Shaun was set back. His old counterpart cleaned up his life. Greg found a direction and pursued a future. The iron was still hot as Shaun continued his alumni search. Bret Jackson's profile was discovered next.

Bret was all state in three sports. His athletic ability enhanced Shaun's image, or so he thought. Bret was Shaun's role model friend. He served as a connection to the popular students in school. Shaun had always behaved in Brett's presence. He had to. The back of the yearbook would have his phone number. Shaun called the Jackson residence.

Mr. Jackson answered the phone. "Good evening, Jackson residence."

Shaun was getting nervous and responded. "Hi, this is Shaun baker; is Brett there?"

"Hello, Shaun," greeted Mr. Jackson. "Our son doesn't live here anymore. He married Sue Colton, and they are now living in Marysville."

This news depressed Shaun. Brett advanced in life, leaving Shaun behind. "Okay, Mr. Johnson," said Shaun "It has been nice talking to you."

"It's nice hearing from you too," said Mr. Jackson. "We wish you the best." The call was ended with Mr. Jackson hanging up. In a frantic pace, Shaun raced through the remainder of the yearbook. He was desperate to salvage any friendships. He reached the last page and found a long shot: Chuck Williams.

Chuck was a farm boy. He worked long hours in fields, helping the family business. Sometimes work had him miss school, which forced him to take summer classes. His isolated lifestyle and quiet demeanor had Shaun befriend him when he was around. Chuck never got into trouble. Shaun found Chuck's phone number and called.

The phone started to ring, and then an automated recording played. It was from the telephone company and stated how the number was disconnected. Shaun remembered that Chuck wanted to go to college. He probably did, with the family moving on. Like the mighty dragon "Puff," Shaun became obsolete and left behind.

"Painted wings and giant springs make way for other toys."

Shaun hit bottom. It seemed that everyone he knew grew up and went away. He was getting old with no development. Depressed and alone, he looked out the window to see his only friends: the constellations.

They were all there waiting for him. If he studied them long enough, they would introduce more friends for Shaun to assemble. He looked at his favorite, "Fairy." There was something different that night. "Fairy's" right arm was extended by glistening stars. It seemed to point at the river below.

Shaun looked down and saw "Fairy's" reflection dance on top of the dark waves. In a split second, a tiny golden light appeared from the distant mountain range. A faint whistle could be heard. It was the train of salvation! The shiny water illuminated the locomotive. It was pulling a few empty flats. This was Shaun's calling, but he had to act fast!

He looked under his bed and pulled out a Cub Scout backpack that had provisions in it.

He put on his jacket and ran into the living room. His grandparents were in their room asleep. He hastily searched drawers and found a pen and paper. He wrote a brief message.

"Grandma and Grandpa, I have to go now. I have a job far away, but I'll be back one day. I love both of you!

Shaun."

He placed the note on the dining room table and left the house with his traveling gear. He ran down a dark path that would reach the railroad tracks. He had the aid of downhill running as the train's presence could be heard. Branches would brush his face as an occasional rock would come out from his footing. The mighty engine and the hissing of pressurized lines grew louder as he sprinted towards his future.

Finally, he reached a clearing where the train was coasting for transients. The metal chariot was larger than life! It was gradually picking up speed as an empty flat car approached. He threw his backpack on the wooden deck and tried to climb the metal ladder that was welded on the frame. As he grabbed the iron rungs, an opened hand came out of the darkness. He clasped it and climbed onto the accelerating flat car. He made it!

His backpack was handed to him by a graying old man. The elder smiled and said, "You must be tuckered out!" He then introduced himself saying, "My name is Harvey."

Shaun caught his breath as he shook hands, introducing himself. "My name is Shaun."

Harvey stared at Shaun and said, "There is lots of work at the end of this line to load these flatcars. They could use a strong young man like you! They even want to hire good help full-time and provide room and board."

Shaun gazed at Harvey and said, "Well good, that's why I'm here!"

The two sat down with the bulkhead serving as a backrest. The train blew its whistle as it headed for the mountains. He rested his head against the bulkhead and looked up to the heavens. He wanted to thank his friends for direction.

The top of the reinforced barrier served as a paint roller for the galaxy. One by one, his friends crossed above him showing that they would always be there. "Fairy," "Spaceman," "Twinkle," and the cast of many others seemed to guide the train. Like his great grandfather, Shaun was going to the new world! What was more important, he was needed and already made his first friend.

# THE POOR CULTURE

THE MEETING ENDED with corporate heads nodding in approval. It was now time for Craig Lions to perform. He would serve as chauffeur and drive the executives to the airport.

Craig always filled in the gaps at the factory. He was that "extra" who did the dirty work. His unlimited chores included acting as secretary, driver, janitor, and mail boy. Craig's presence at company meetings was always questioned. He was needed one way, but outcast another. There was more to his life, though. Unbeknownst to him, this humble man held a unique status in society.

Craig drove corporate CEO Alex Sampson and his entourage to the airport. He maintained his "speak when spoken to" policy. The departure was quick; he drove up to the gate and quietly parked the car. He opened the trunk and handed luggage to his passengers.

The company brass thanked the driver and left.

Dust was settling in the plant now that the "Gestapo" was gone. The aftermath would result in new policies and deadlines.

The rest of the day would involve a conference between plant manager Daniel Foster and vice president, Stan Byres.

"Why do you allow Craig Lions to attend these meetings?" asked Stan Byers.

Daniel Foster leaned back in his chair. He placed his cigar in an ashtray and said, "He's a trusted servant."

"He seems out of place at those meetings. He just sits there and doesn't get involved," Stan observed.

"Craig is involved," said Daniel. "When we need to document information from those meetings, Craig's mind is a steel trap. He stays within his boundaries and catches us if we forget anything. Craig will also do the odds-and-ends that are needed around here, and without complaining. He knows his place."

"But, Craig isn't one of us," the vice president rebutted.

Daniel looked off into the distance as he thought. "I have to agree with you," he said. "That's part of the beauty. He makes a reliable designated driver for our luncheons and cocktail parties. He will also address disgruntled employees who we don't want to waste our time with. We don't actually hang out with him; he's there for us." The plant manager looked at Stan and grinned.

Stan understood the cleverness of the situation. "I get it!" he replied.

A knock was heard on the door.

"Come in," said the plant manager.

It was Craig. "Here are the keys to the company car," he said to Daniel.

"Why don't you hang on to them and have lunch with us?" suggested Daniel.

"That would be great!" replied Craig.

"We'll meet in the parking lot in a few minutes," said Daniel. Craig acknowledged his statement and left.

Stan gazed at Daniel, realizing he was talking in code. Craig would serve as the designated driver for the two managers. Daniel winked at Stan as they shared a secret. They left for lunch.

The three men were seated at the restaurant. The server greeted the table and asked if they wanted any drinks.

"I'll have a beer," said Daniel.

"I will have one, too," said Stan.

Like a well-trained dog, Craig knew his place. "Water will be fine," he said.

The two bosses made eye contact and smiled.

When lunch was finished, they paid the bill and went to the parking lot. The mission to return to the plant was interrupted as a woman in the parking lot confronted Craig.

"Please!" she begged. "We are out of food and need money to buy groceries! I am a single mother, and my children are starving!"

Craig looked at the desperate woman. He then looked at her three innocent children and saw the hope in their eyes. He opened his wallet and handed her what money he had.

"Thank you!" cried the woman as she hugged him. "Thank you very much; God will bless you for this!"
The woman left.

There was a moment of silence as the co-workers absorbed what happened.

Stan spoke out. "That's your problem right there!"

It was Daniel's turn. "He's right. You are that 'nice guy' who will always finish last! That's why you don't advance in life; your job is a classic example of that."

Stan continued. "This isn't the first time we have witnessed this. Those types of people prey on people like you. You are that sucker who will work every day and give it all away to those panhandlers. Those beggars who you give money to are the ones who leave shopping carts on the sidewalks! They are all members of the poor culture, and they see you as one of them!"

Craig got angry. "I'm just doing what I was taught. My parents always gave to needy, and so will I!"

They entered the car and drove in silence.

Craig would spend the rest of his day cleaning the room where the meeting was held.

That evening, karma would reach out to him. He was pushing a grocery cart in the store when a rugged man approached him.

"Sir," called out the tattooed man. "That's my sister over there." He pointed towards a woman with three children. He recognized them as the family he helped that day. They came up to Craig and hugged him.

"That was pretty cool what you did for them today," he said. "Those guys you were with don't care for people the way you do. I am grateful that you still cared for my sister and her children."

The man introduced himself to Craig. "My name is Rick, and you are always welcome in our home."

The two shook hands as Craig made a new friend.

The following day, work resumed as normal. Craig kept busy tying up loose ends. Shortly after lunch, he was summoned to Daniel Foster's office. The plant manager had a stern look on his face when Craig arrived.

"We need you to drive an employee home," said Daniel. "Terry Walden claims to feel sick and requested to be sent home. There are rumors floating around that he has a drinking problem."

Craig was devastated. "I will be glad to give him a ride home," he said.

Daniel gave Craig the keys to the company car. "You can take your time driving him home," said Daniel. "You seem to have a friendship with him; maybe you can find out if he has a problem."

Craig met Terry in the parking lot. They entered the car and began to drive. Craig spoke first. "Are you okay, Terry?"

"I am starting to feel better," Terry answered.

"Can I talk to you about something personal?" asked Craig.

"Craig, you are the only office person that I will talk to," said Terry. "Go ahead."

"I respect you as a person," said Craig. "I love you as a friend. There are signs that you are an alcoholic, like my sister. I will sometimes join her at her alcohol meetings as a support. They have counselors there who professionally evaluate anyone who is affected by this disease. We are attending a pot luck dinner at their hall tonight. Why don't you join us for dinner? You can be our guest and listen to their program."

Terry sat back in the car and let the information register. "I do have an alcohol problem," he said. "There is something special about you, Craig. Normally, an employee would be offended to hear such an accusation from a salary person. I would be honored to spend an evening with you and your sister!"

Craig smiled at Terry and shook his hand. They agreed to attend the meeting that night. Craig and his sister would pick up Terry at five o'clock and go to the pot luck.

Five o'clock arrived with a friendly knock on Terry's door. It was Craig and his sister, Janet. Craig introduced his sister to Terry, and the three left for the meeting. Upon arriving, Terry recognized several of his friends. Craig said, "That happens all the time. I have bumped into many friends and neighbors here myself. We all belong!"

Terry felt accepted. The evening would be a new beginning in Terry's life. He was inspired by motivational speakers and was relieved to see many who shared his problem.

The pasta dish Craig brought enhanced the feast. Dinner was a Thanksgiving with the entire fellowship holding hands and saying grace. Terry joined the community that night.

Friday was mundane for Craig. He attended several meetings and walked the plant in search of anything that needed to be fixed, refilled, or replaced. He would eventually cross paths with every member of the work force. This was his favorite aspect of the job. He got to visit with others and express his care for them.

Before quitting time, Craig was summoned to Daniel Foster's office. Craig entered.

"Alex Sampson is coming into town this Saturday. Will you be available to drive us out for dinner in the company car?" asked Daniel.

"That will be my pleasure," said Craig.

"We'll be discussing important matters over dinner and will be there for several hours," said Daniel.

Craig understood what Mr. Foster meant. He was to drive the clients to dinner and wait for them in the car. "How about I bring my cell phone and wait in the car?" suggested Craig.

"That sounds best," said Daniel. "We will meet here at six o'clock Saturday night.

On Saturday, Craig dressed formally and arrived a half hour early. He had the company car clean and ready to go. The dinner party was meeting in Daniel Foster's office. At six o'clock, they left the office and walked toward the waiting car. Craig opened the car doors for his passengers.

"To Brandie's Broiler, and make it quick," said Daniel.

Craig nodded his head and drove to the most expensive restaurant in town. He pulled up to the prestigious landmark and provided valet parking. He would wait nearby for their phone call. Several hours would pass.

It was past nine o'clock when Craig's cell phone rang. The drunk patrons, along with a noisy background, made communication difficult.

"Where are you, Craig?" asked Daniel Foster.

"I am one block away and can be there in less than a minute," responded Craig.

"We actually want to walk to the car. We have sat down so long that a brief walk sounds good," said Daniel.

Craig was parked in an alley just one block away and gave directions. He disconnected his cell phone and waited. The management elite were soon in view. They stumbled from the effects of drinking as a loud conversation full of laughter could be heard. Craig got out of the car and opened the doors. Danger struck.

The alley was infiltrated with thugs. They could see that the well-dressed driver was waiting for others who would possibly have valuables.

"Everybody lay down!" yelled a silhouette. The company men saw that they were surrounded by exposed weapons and an unknown amount of assailants. Then came passion.

"Hey!" cried out one of the robbers. "Is that Craig?"

"It is!" confirmed another masked figure.

"We're sorry, Craig," said a distant male voice. "We didn't know that it was you and your friends."

"Don't look," instructed the first man. "We are leaving; just stay down for one minute." The would-be victims remained face down for several minutes. Finally, Craig got up and looked around. They were safe. He said, "They're gone."

Alex Sampson got up and looked at Craig in bewilderment. He said, "You seem to know a lot of people in this town!"

Daniel Foster said, "I'll call the police!"

"You don't have to," said Alex. "Craig is enough."

The relieved party dusted the dirt off of their suits and entered the car. Craig drove them back to the plant.

Monday would be dedicated to diplomacy. The plant had agreed to hold a conference for community relations. Mayor Higgins and the Attorney General would attend. This would be a long day for Daniel Foster and Alex Sampson.

The morning started off with a presentation about the environment and local charities. Plant tours would be next. They would embark in small groups led by Craig. While this was happening, the plant manager would have an open-door policy throughout the day. The conference room would have refreshments.

Craig took the first tour through the plant. Daniel went to his office with Alex, leaving his door open.

The plant manager received his first visitor. It was a rugged tattooed man wearing a jean vest. He introduced himself as Rick.

Daniel was intimidated by the man's appearance. He shook hands as he introduced himself to Rick.

"How do you know of this place?" asked Daniel.

"This is the only good job in town," said Rick. "Everybody wants to work here."

"Have you applied to work here?" asked the plant manager.

"Many times," Rick answered. "This community knows that you are unfair in hiring. You only pick friends and relatives. A local like myself doesn't have a chance."

Daniel blushed in embarrassment. "We have made many improvements around here!" he insisted.

"You only have one good element in this factory," said Rick.

Daniel was curious and asked what it was.

"Craig Lions," Rick declared. "He actually cares about everyone in this town. My neighbors respect him because he has given to many families. He treats everybody with respect."

Rick made his point and left. Daniel and Alex looked at each other in astonishment.

Moments later, a second visitor arrived. It was Terry Walden's wife.

"Come in, Mrs. Walden," greeted Daniel.

She entered the room and addressed the two managers. "I wanted to thank this company for helping my husband," she said. "He is now in treatment for his problem. He also has a new outlook in life. The fellowship Craig took him to was what was missing in his life. He is happy because he found a new direction. I just wanted to come by and thank you for helping Terry."

The grateful woman hugged the two men and left. Again, Daniel and Alex stared at one another in shock. They realized that Craig had acted alone.

Like the ghosts that visited Ebenezer Scrooge, they would get one more visit on this subject matter.

A rough looking group of men approached the open door with a basket. The oldest one asked if they could enter.

"Please come in!" said Daniel Foster.

"We need to talk," said one of them.

The voice seemed familiar. It then occurred to the two executives that these men were the assailants from Saturday night. Fear was in the room.

"You don't know us, but that's not important," continued the stranger. "We are here to make peace." He handed Daniel a basket that held wine, cheeses, and crackers.

The CEO and plant manager looked at the gift and kept quiet.

"We like Craig," said the leader. "That man accepts everybody in the community. Where we live, we have a tradition. If you have extra food, you light a candle and leave it in the window. It means that you can feed a hungry neighbor. You also have those who bring food when they visit. Most importantly, you make a friend for life. Craig is always welcomed in every home that has a candle. He is our neighbor, and we love him."

Daniel and Alex sat still and continued to listen.

"Somebody made a comment about shopping carts in the streets," said the leader. "That's done on purpose. The supermarkets give two dollars for every cart returned. We place them throughout the neighborhood for anyone who needs money. We never litter, but we will pick it up."

The leader removed a plastic bag from his pocket. He placed it on the plant manager's desk. It was full of cigarette butts, the expensive brand that Daniel Foster smoked. "This is litter!" said the leader. "And cigarettes are bad for you!"

The spokesman left the butts on the desk. He shook hands with the executives and departed. Daniel and Alex left the room, going in opposite directions. They had to think about the events that just happened.

Daniel and Alex soon reunited in the office to finish out the day. There would be more visitors. They agreed to keep the responses about Craig to themselves. They would, however, offer to take Craig out to dinner. It would simply be a nice visit to get to know him better. Craig accepted.

They went to a Mexican restaurant close to Craig's home. The three ate dinner, and Craig was the focus of conversation. The bosses were in awe with his humbleness and how grateful he was to have a job. It was getting dark when they finished their meal. They would further honor him by driving to his home first, so he could skip the bus.

They were stunned to see the neighborhood Craig lived in. It was the poor side of town, and the block seemed to be victimized by slum landlords. Craig stopped in front of his residence and got out of the car.

"Thank you for dinner!" said Craig.

"You are welcome!" said Alex.

"I will see you Monday," said Daniel. "Have a good weekend." Daniel shook Craig's hand and got into the driver's seat.

The bosses watched Craig walk up to his apartment and unlock the door. He entered his home and closed the door.

"Drive down the street, turn around, and park," said Alex.

Daniel did as Alex instructed.

They faced his apartment and studied Craig's standard of living. They could see the happy employee through his living room window.

The two continued to survey the environment. There were homes that still had Christmas lights on them. Shopping carts were thoughtfully placed in convenient locations, and certain windows had lit candles. Craig's home life would now begin. He placed a lit candle in front of his window.

"What should we do for him?" Daniel asked Alex.

"Nothing," replied the CEO. "That would ruin everything; he's a self-made man, just like us."

Moments later, an elderly couple across the street left their home with a steaming kettle. Soon, a young man left his dwelling wearing kitchen gloves and holding a hot tray. Another neighbor walked down the street with a loaf of bread. All went to Craig's front door.

The wealthy bosses viewed Craig's living room window as the "poor culture" continued to arrive. Smiles accompanied handshakes and hugs. More friends showed up bringing more food.

"Do you have friends like that?" Alex asked Daniel.

Daniel thought for a moment and said, "No."

"I don't, either," Alex said softly.

Alex looked at Daniel and spoke again. "You see, he is the only person in town who can go anywhere. There are no streets or alleys that restrict him. He has no curfew. Craig Lions definitely has the 'key' to this community. That's because he shows respect to everyone. In turn, he is loved and welcomed in every home."

The two men continued to monitor Craig's personal life. They felt incomplete. There was something missing in their world. They exceeded in business, and that led to elite statuses and places in high society. That lifestyle demanded a separation of classes. In Craig Lion's life, there was no separation of classes; everyone belonged. In turn, he belonged everywhere.

Craig Lions only wanted to be happy, and he was. That gave him a peace within himself, making him a rich man.

# THE ESSAY

JACKIE HALL SMILED as the debate team entered the bus. The retired truck driver seemed to have a new life. He felt revitalized serving as a full-time counselor for local youth groups. This cause would help alleviate the secret pain this father of one endured. His own daughter was not in his life.

"Good morning, Jackie!" said each child as they boarded.

He seemed to have been "adopted." They respected him as an adult but addressed him as a friend.

"Good morning!" Jackie would respond.

When the last seat belt buckled, Jackie announced, "Here we go!" The happy cargo cheered as the field trip was underway. The conscientious driver watched the road while using a mirror to view his passengers.

He would look at the dashboard and gaze at a picture of his daughter. Jackie would fight back the tears, wishing she was here.

The bus arrived at the crosstown high school. This was a special occasion. It was an awards ceremony to honor the many literary achievements that came from local scholars.

Mrs. Wellington greeted the pupils when they arrived in the parking lot. She was the leader of the debate team and would escort them to the auditorium.

"Thank you, Jackie!" said every child as they left the bus.

"You are welcome!" said the bus driver. "Have a wonderful time; I will be here to drive you back."

The auditorium was full of  students that represented the region. Many plaques and trophies covered a table near the podium. This would be a grand event.

The festivities moved swiftly as awards were presented, followed by applause. The climax of the ceremony was to honor an essay that acquired national recognition. This piece of literature was a challenge for all parents, to be parents. It encouraged every parent to go beyond their families and serve every child they could.

Mayor Higgens read the inspiring essay to the audience. When finished, the entire room stood up and cheered. He then displayed a plaque that was to be awarded to the author of this inspirational writing.

Mayor Higgens announced, "I am proud to present this award to our own Jackie Hall!"

The room gasped in shock as everyone's favorite bus driver received the event's highest award. All stood up and gave a five minute ovation. Jackie entered the stage and shook hands with the mayor. He accepted the plaque and held it over his head. He then faced the crowd with his famous smile.

The essay would reach out to magazines and newsletters. The former truck driver was achieving a celebrity status. Charitable organizations throughout the nation would publish the essay. Many invited Jackie to attend conventions, conferences, and to give talks at non-profit fund-raisers. Inspired readers made contact, with some becoming pen pals.

Jackie felt good inside. He was encouraging parents to secure a relationship with their children. He also drew much-needed attention to those that were abandoned. Still, it seemed he had a void that would never be filled.

A particular internet pen pal seemed to be extra special to Jackie. Her "handle" was "Lostangel" and identified herself as a woman that found it hard to forgive her father. She would point out that he missed too much of her childhood and believed that he didn't care. Jackie's compassion would console this "mystery woman." He wanted to know what her father did for a living. She would write that he traveled far away- and was seldom home. She couldn't accept that he had a career that caused him to miss most of her childhood.

This dilemma struck a nerve with Jackie; he knew what it was like to be in her father's situation. "JackieHall" wrote back using his life as a trucker to express what her father must have gone through.

151

"When I married, I didn't want to drive a truck anymore," wrote Jackie. "I wanted to get a job in town and be home every night. We lived in a small community that didn't have good jobs. When I became a father, I had to earn more. I had no choice but to make a living by driving. If I asked for time off, my boss would threaten to replace me. I "had" to drive those long hours. I paid a horrible price for being away. I missed out on almost everything and eventually divorced. The worst part is that it cost me my daughter. That's why I wrote the essay. I don't want anybody else to know the pain that comes with losing your own child. Your father was probably in the same predicament as I was, with the same regrets."

There was a long pause- then came a response. "Can you tell me about her?"

"JackieHall" began to type. "She is the most wonderful gift I have ever received from God. She always made me happy. I cherished every night I was home and always read her a bedtime story. She made me a Father's Day mug when she was ten; it's the only cup I will ever drink out of. I carry her picture at all times; when I drive, it's always on the dashboard."

"LosTangel" typed another question. "What's her name?"

Jackie wrote, "Laura." I call her, "Angel" though, because she's Heaven sent!"

"Where is she now?" wrote the pen pal.

"My daughter is with her mom's family," wrote Jackie. "They look at me as a father that didn't care and hate me for that."

The communication came to an abrupt end with the retired trucker signing off.

The following day, Jackie attended a luncheon for Big Brothers of America. His recent success made him a popular guest speaker. He would read his famous essay and visit with young men and fellow counselors. There was always an ovation after his speech and pictures taken with new acquaintances. Jackie lived for this cause. It helped make him feel like the dad he should have been. The day also had another importance; he would write "LosTangel."

Jackie Hall arrived home and had dinner with his sister. The siblings were always close through their upbringing. When each divorced, they continued their happy childhood by living together. It was a warm household.

"How was the Big Brother's luncheon today?" asked Diana Hall.

"It was wonderful," answered the brother. "There were many fatherless boys that just need that one big chance. I hope that my visit helped some of them."

"You probably helped all of them," remarked the sister.

"I appreciate dinner," said Jackie. "I am going to check my e-mails now." The brother then went to his room and turned on the computer.

Within moments, a message from "LosTangel" appeared. Soon, they were corresponding.

Jackie started to write first. "I want to apologize for hanging up on you last night. It seems that I still can't face the reality of my daughter's absence. I always get depressed over it."

"That's okay," responded the pen pal. "I realize that it takes a lot out of you. How was your day?"

Jackie began to write her about the Big Brother's function and of the many boys he met that day. "They were all abandoned and only need one reason to strive for success. It just takes one caring adult to change their life."

"LosTangel" wrote a question. "What makes you care for children that aren't yours?"

"I am surprised with you," wrote "JackieHall". "You read my essay about families. We are all related to one another, and it's everyone's responsibility to go the extra mile for any child left out! That especially goes for dads like me- that weren't always there for their own children. I am ashamed that I failed my daughter! At least I am doing whatever I can, for as many children as possible."

The pen pal answered. "I have to agree with your logic."

The weekend was coming up and Jackie asked if she had any plans.

"My girlfriends and I will go out on Saturday night and celebrate Cinco de Mayo," she responded.

"I thought you were of Hispanic origin," wrote Jackie. "I bet you have a beautiful dress for your holiday and will dance all night long!"

"What's your family background?" wrote "LosTangel".

"We are of Irish decent," answered Jackie. "The people from the community I live in are all from the "old country." We represent the farmers and truck drivers that live here."

Jackie had to check other e-mails. He received mail everyday that addressed him as a youth counselor. His dedication to this cause had him answer everyone that made contact. He said his good-byes to the pen pal. "I will be here for you tomorrow," he wrote.

"I will be here before my outing," she answered.

Friday was a routine day for Jackie. He assisted on one field trip and served in the cafeteria and detention office. He looked forward to another visit with "LosTangel" when he got home.

After dinner, he went to his computer and was happy to find her waiting. "Are you ready for the big dance?" he wrote.

"Almost," she responded. "How was your day?"

Jackie briefly wrote her about his day at the school. "It was a little mundane but I still loved it! Next weekend will be great though."

"What makes next weekend so special?" she wrote.

"We are initiating new counselors for the local youth groups," he answered. "This is where you meet people that care. They believe in our cause for helping troubled youth. It enhances the foundation needed to nurture this problem. The more people that step up, the more success we'll have."

"What are the qualifications to become a counselor ?" she typed.

"We only ask for the basics," he wrote. "A high school diploma or GED and  a clean record will grant anyone an interview. It boils down to how much you really care for children."

"What does a counselor do?" asked the pen pal.

"Everything imaginable," replied Jackie. "There are field trips, team sports, picnics, ice cream socials, dances, camping, and listening to their problems. We also want to know a child's dream and help them get there. These kids seem to adopt us, with many being a part of our lives forever. It's a beautiful world! May I ask what you do for a living?"

"I don't know what I want to do for a career yet," she typed.

"Do you want to spend next weekend with us?" asked Jackie. "You seem to be exactly what we need for this program. You can join in all the festivities and meet people- who are just like you!"

"That sound's wonderful, but I have no where to stay," replied the woman.

"I live with my sister, and we have a guest room," wrote Jackie. "You are welcomed to stay with us as long as you want.
"I would like that," answered "LosTangel." "How about I meet you at this seminar; I know who you are."

"That would be great," he responded. "I must be a "marked man;" you know who I am- and I will find out who you are!"

Jackie e-mailed her a newsletter that gave information about the function. He wrote, "We will keep in touch and look forward to meeting you."

Sunday night continued with "JackieHall" finding "LosTangel" on the internet.

Jackie initiated the visit. "How many hearts did you break last night?"

"At least a few that I am aware of," answered the invisible friend. "Will you tell me more about your life?"

"What do you want to know?" he wrote.

"I have a question," she wrote . "If you could have any wish, what would it be?"

He responded, "I have thought about that many times. I wish that my only career would have been a youth counselor - despite the low pay. I would have been everything I could have been  for other children, with my daughter  involved. Then, she never would have lost her dad." "JackieHall" signed off and dissipated.

Monday was a travel day for Jackie. He was to speak at a convention for the Boy Scouts and Girl Scouts of America. This assembly would last all day, with the famous counselor inspiring all with his essay. He eventually returned home to enjoy dinner with his sister and to visit with "LosTangel."

"I have to apologize for walking out on you again last night," he wrote his pen pal.

"That's okay," she typed. "I now have a better understanding of the pain you go through missing Laura. May I take the risk of asking another sensitive question?"

"Go ahead," wrote Jackie. "I will try to have the strength to answer."

"What was it like driving for days at a time away from your family?" she inquired.

There was a long pause that built up to his answer. "I felt like I was a soldier on a mission. I went far away to protect what I lived for. There were times when I thought that I wasn't going to make it back home."

"What do you mean?" asked "LosTangel."

Jackie responded, "I was once in a bad accident where I was pried out of my truck and read my last rights. I didn't want my wife to know what happened. I told her that I had to accept an emergency long haul that would keep the company in business. My wife yelled at me over the phone and threatened to divorce me. I prayed to God and lived through that ordeal. I spent three weeks in the hospital. I had to take out loans to buy a new truck. When my wife saw my new truck, she left me thinking that I only cared about myself. I had to work longer to pay those bills."

There was a pause in Jackie's writing as he continued. "There were times when starving families pleaded with me at truck stops. Sometimes, I gave

158

them what little I had. There were times when I wanted to give something but had nothing to give. That would haunt me for days. I have had mechanical breakdowns that took all my money. Bad weather, snow, ice and floods had me stranded in towns where nobody knew me. I had to live in my truck and starve. Many nights, I cried realizing that I had failed my family."

The pen pal signed off for the night without responding. Jackie finished the evening by reading his mail and answering inquiries.

The rest of the week was dedicated to various activities surrounding youth programs. Basketball, badminton, and volleyball tournaments would consume most of Jackie's schedule. Home life would change as the brother and sister prepared for their guest.

Once home, Jackie and Diana enjoyed a warm dinner together. Diana provided fresh bedding for the guest room as Jackie vacuumed and dusted. They smiled at each other with the anticipation of their new friend. The brother always told his sister about writing to the woman known as "LosTangel." The two felt she was special and wanted her as a house guest. "JackieHall" would now message "LosTangel."

Like "Old faithful," she was there.

"We are ready for you!" wrote Jackie.

"I can't wait to get there!" answered the pen pal.
She continued. "I owe you an apology this time. I lost my emotions over our last visit and had to walk away. What you said about your true life as a truck driver affected me."

"I didn't mean to hurt you in anyway," typed Jackie. "I told you things that nobody else knows about."

"I realize that," she replied. "I must admit, you are a great speaker."

"How would you know that?" asked Jackie.

"I have attended several functions that featured you as a guest speaker," admitted the unseen follower. "You actually care about others! Many are inspired by you, including me. I read the newsletter you mailed me about this weekend. I will be there and introduce myself. I will watch you read your essay again and change lives!"

Jackie was overwhelmed! His secret pen pal had been in auditoriums where he spoke. She knew him very well. Their communication would last a few more minutes. "LosTangel" typed that she would not write anymore that week. The next "meeting" would be the actual visit on Saturday. "JackieHall" could hardly wait!

Saturday arrived. Jackie would be accompanied by his sister as they left for the convention center. Once they got in the parking lot, the storied youth counselor was recognized by many. The moment he left his car, many hands extended to be shook, with pictures being taken. Carefully, he and his sister looked about trying to identify their new house guest.

They had little information to go on. They were looking for a Hispanic woman- who knew who he was. On occasion, such a profile would be spotted. The big, bright smile of the Irish truck driver approached the few candidates, only to be mistaken. None of the women knew of a "LosTangel." The siblings finally entered the building where more picture poses and handshakes awaited. The ceremony was about to start, with Jackie headlining the event. His nationally acclaimed essay would reach out to everyone present. The new counselors would then get on stage and be sworn into service by Jackie.

Jackie was handed the list of the new counselors he would inaugurate. He was pleasantly surprised to see "LosTangel" as the last cadet to be certified. This motivated him to give the best performance he ever gave as a speaker. In reciting his essay, the room sat quietly in tears. When he finished, he received a standing ovation that seemed like an eternity. He then spoke to the audience about loving God's children. He emphasized self-sacrifice, by putting all children first. He then told the story about his past life as a father who was wasn't there enough. He pointed out that he could have been involved with this program years ago. He said that the guarantee of being close to your family was beyond making a lot of money. He said that his own child became a victim, just like the children in the youth programs. He shared what life had taught him: every adult's life should be a continuous sacrifice for all children.

The room stood up and gave the retired truck driver another ovation. "And now," announced Jackie, "it's time to give this world more youth counselors !" The room cheered as the recruits took stage. The last person to enter the stage was a woman in dark sunglasses. She wore a gorgeous Mexican dress with a matching hat. Jackie smiled in approval as the woman smiled back.

The master of ceremonies read each name. He then had the individual hold up his or her right hand and pledge the oath. When he reached the final recruit, he announced her name, "LosTangel."

There was silence as the woman said, "That's not my name."

"Is it misspelled here?" asked Jackie.

"Not really," she answered. "The letters are right. My first name is actually the first four words, not the first three."

"Forgive me," said Jackie as he studied the perplexed spelling.

The orator then took "LosTangel" and changed it to..."Lost angel." He thought for a moment and could only think of his own angel: Laura. The father cautiously removed his eyes from the script and looked at the woman standing before him. Her hat and glasses were now off. He recognized her beautiful blue eyes and flowing auburn hair. He trembled with the realization that he was with his daughter again!

"I want my daddy back," said the proud daughter. "I promise to share you with other children. I want to live with you and help children that don't know their fathers, but I know mine!"

It took all of Jackie Hall's strength to announce "Laura Hall" as the final youth counselor to be sworn in. She raised her right hand and pledged her oath. She then hugged her father and said, "I love you, dad!"

The trembling man hugged his child while he looked up in tears. He thanked God for this second chance. In relief, he kissed the top of her head saying, "I love you, Angel; welcome home!"

## Your Mother Should Know

LESLIE BRANDON SAT STILL as the fitting took place. He was wearing the experimental "control helmet" for the first time. This prototype was designed to allow hot furnaces to be monitored from a distance. If this idea proved successful, it would reduce his department down to one person. It would also have an unnatural bi-product. It would provide him a "sixth" sense that only women have.

The concept of having a laser beam attached to a helmet could target any heat source. The light beam would transfer information that would result in "on-the-spot" adjustments. The helmet also had another feature. It reported information where any heat source was outside its settings and promptly alerted the operator. His command would serve like a polygraph test, having thought move an instrument.

"Is it 'me?'" asked Leslie as he displayed the new "hat."

"It's you!" laughed the head of the Public Relations Department, Marcie Joplin.

The helmet looked like a child's birthday present adorned with ornaments. The custom fit was specifically designed for Leslie and molded to carry sensors.

"We need to test it now," said Plant Manager Robert Greene. "We will spend this afternoon with the engineers that built this. They will show you what this can do and how to operate it."

Leslie took off the control helmet and handed it to Robert Greene.

"We'll meet in the shop after lunch," said the plant manager.

Minutes after lunch ended, Leslie arrived in the shop. Robert Greene was already there with the helmet. He introduced Leslie to a three-man engineering team that would tutor him. They were, "Allen," "Mike," and "Joe." They took him to a private room accompanied with their invention. State-of-the-art controls and gauges were displayed on the opposite side of the room. They were compatible to the command of the new helmet.

The team fitted Leslie with a glove that had sensors covering several fingers. Together, the glove and helmet would allow Leslie's thoughts and his vision to adjust the instruments on the far wall.

"And now, we'll turn it on," said Allen. "Sit down."

Allen bent over Leslie once he sat down. He flipped a tiny switch on the back side of the helmet. A brief tingling sensation could be felt through the gloved hand as the interior of the helmet gave a temporary mild vibration. He relaxed as a "radiant sensation" seemed to travel throughout his body.

Joe wore the traditional glasses and white coat. He addressed Leslie. "All you have to do is direct the laser to the panel you wish to control and think."

"How about adjusting the gauge on the far right," suggested Mike. "Let's raise that process temperature from four hundred degrees to five hundred degrees."

Leslie aimed the beam and watched it penetrate the box. He simply thought about "five hundred degrees," and it increased one hundred degrees! Like the evilness of an Ouija board's power, it responded!

His face was expressionless and turned pitch white. He slowly turned towards the three men as they smiled in recognition.

"It's not what you think," said Allen. "Do you think that a polygraph is the devil?"

Leslie thought for a while and shook his head sideways.

"Do you think the technology of a laser beam adjusting a gauge is evil?" asked Allen.

Leslie thought for a while and gave the same response.

"We have simply combined the two," proclaimed Allen.

166

Leslie was relieved that this modern technology was just that. He said a prayer for reassurance, and the first omen came.

Mrs. Keeling entered the room without knocking. She walked up to Leslie and said, "Take that off right now; you have no business playing with that!" The stern bookkeeper gave a vicious stare at Leslie and left.

The men stared at one another not knowing what to think of the interruption. They shrugged their shoulders and continued the trial.

Leslie was to spend the rest of the day mastering the new tool.

The work day ended with Robert Greene entering the room. The "mad professors" expressed their appreciation working with Leslie. The helmet and glove were removed and inspected by the team.

"We'll continue testing first thing tomorrow," said the plant manager.

When Leslie left the plant to get in his car, a strange phenomenon happened. He felt a presence of affection. He looked behind him to see Marcie Joplin. He "knew" at that moment that she secretly admired him. Her facial expression changed into shock- as she realized he could "sense" it. The woman immediately vacated the parking lot out of embarrassment. She got in her car and sped away before Leslie could acknowledge her.

Leslie was dumbfounded. He had never felt that "odd feeling" that revealed another persons' hidden emotion before. This awareness continued when he stopped at the grocery store on the way home. His favorite checker avoided him the moment he entered the store. She usually insisted on serving him at her register. Today, she left as he entered.

The next morning, he met the engineers and plant manager in the shop.

"Our guys have replaced some of the gauges in the refractory last night," said Robert. "They have been updated to correspond with that dome you'll be wearing. I want you to spend all day with the engineers on this project."

Mike fitted the helmet on Leslie and handed him the electronic glove. Once suited, the helmet was activated, and they left for the foundry.

The warm, tingling sensation penetrated Leslie's body like the day before. The mild vibration massaged his scalp and gradually dissipated. He was now armed for battle.

The foursome would walk the entire length of the factory to reach the furnaces. Their travels would pass by the break room. Then it happened. A peculiar feeling overcame Leslie. He detected hatred. George Williams was leaving the break room and noticed Leslie.

George continued to walk away as Leslie felt unwanted vibes from the aging foreman. He understood that he was jealous of his popularity throughout the plant. That hurt Leslie. He always held the up-most respect for that man and considered him a friend. He then noticed that this discovery was different from the ones he had yesterday. George wasn't aware that Leslie "knew."

Leslie wondered, "Is it different with women?"

The question was answered immediately. Leslie looked at the office across the breezeway. Women were staring at him through the windows in disbelief. "They" knew that he acquired a special trait that was forbidden to the race of men.

The test pilot continued his trek to the foundry.

The morning was successful. Everything worked at Leslie's will. Lunchtime arrived quickly, and with it- a surprise. The office girls wanted to take Leslie out for dinner that night. The "man of the hour" accepted. They were to meet at "Darcy's Grill" at seven that evening: their treat. He would continue the day sharpshooting commands from the control helmet.

He arrived for dinner at the designated time and was greeted by Marcie at the front door. She welcomed him and led him back to the banquet room. Every woman from the plant was there. Leslie was the only male. His new "gift" made the scrutiny directed at him unmistakable.

"We have a test," said Carmen Rodregis. She got up and said, "Follow me." Leslie and a few others followed Carmen to the bar. She sat in the back and pointed at a man sitting alone at the edge of the counter. "What do you think he's feeling right now?" she whispered.

Leslie studied the stranger and watched him leave for the restroom and return. He eventually said, "He's in pain! That man doesn't want to live anymore!"

Carmen looked at the women that shared the table and said, "He's got it all right!" The girls then introduced themselves to the man and listened to him. Leslie understood that his "male presence" would give a worse effect. He returned to the banquet room.

"Leslie," called out Monica Hills. "Would you come here for a moment?"

Leslie cautiously approached Monica.

"I want to ask you a question," she said. She pointed at a small box on the table. "Can you tell us what's inside the box?"

Leslie stared at the box and concentrated. He then looked at Monica and said, "I have no idea."

Kate Florance asked, "Could you take a guess?"

"Okay," said Leslie. "A doughnut?" he guessed. "How about a necklace or a napkin?" he questioned.

Monica opened the box to reveal its contents. It was her cell phone.

"Well, that's a good sign," said Kate. "At least you don't have more than us."

Leslie sat down and looked at the dinner menu. Soon, all placed their order with the server.

Sue Johnson pointed at Leslie telling the server, "I am buying for him."

Dinner was served. The guest was always respected at work and the evening blossomed into a fun occasion. During the meal, the women noticed a change in Leslie. He wasn't "picking-up" on their feelings anymore. The spell wore off! It seemed that the "Gizmo" he wore at work could only advance him temporary.

The evening continued with the women thanking Leslie for attending. They let him know that he experienced a sense that was only meant for females.

"A man would use it to conquer," said Darla Martin.

"I agree," said the entire room.

Darla continued, "It's actually a type of radar, that enables a woman to better understand a man, and nurture.

"Right," exclaimed the room.

"Leslie, we love you," said Lee Bushing. "If there was a man that should have this gift, it would be you!"

The women then cheered in approval of Leslie.

"You are still a man though, and it isn't meant for you either," said Joan Easily.

One-by-one, the women agreed.

"You are a compassionate man," pointed out Ruth Myers. "This new technology is designed to reduce jobs. You wouldn't want to be a part of that, would you?" The room silenced with the fear loved ones losing their job.

Leslie would allow this vital information to digest. He enjoyed the remainder of the evening and eventually went home. He couldn't sleep that night. He stayed up for hours trying to fathom the "power" he had with this new radar.

The next day, Leslie was eager to start work and get "energized." He learned that the treatments only gave temporary ability. He would purposely wear the helmet the entire shift to test its longevity. He would further incorporate this into his personal life.

He started off his day continuing the experiment.
The testing was flawless. A corporate decision would soon be addressed to transfer the entire operation to this new technology. If it was approved, many jobs would be lost. Leslie lost his compassion for fellow workers. He stopped caring.

The women that graced him the night before were appalled. Their co-worker was guilty of treason. They were ashamed of him. Worst yet, they were afraid for him. Each knew that the other had the intuition to communicate this problem. He would still bi-pass their advice, to venture deeper. His ability to read the feelings of friends at work caused pain. He became distant, without the "guys" knowing why.

He would search for answers in his private life.

It was now quitting time. He stormed out of the plant without talking to anyone. His destination was his neighborhood bar. He would hurry to have full use of his temporary power. Within thirty minutes, he was at "Larry's Tavern." He entered the bar.

There was a haze of contradiction. Smiles greeted him with handshakes. Some were sincere, and others weren't. Larry, himself, approached his regular customer. It hit Leslie like a ton of bricks; Larry didn't actually like him. Larry still smiled at the patron and extended his hand. Leslie glared at his "friend" and left quietly. Larry couldn't understand the rejection and followed Leslie to the parking lot. It was too late; he was already in his car and left.

His next stop would be his girlfriend Cheryl's house. Earlier that day, he told her that he would be out of town on a business trip. He wanted to spy on her to see if she was faithful. Her thoughts encompassed him as he pulled up in front of her home. She was alone but didn't miss him. The loyal woman admired a neighbor and wanted to date him. Her relationship with Leslie was that of a mother trying to raise a son. She wanted to be free of Leslie. Now he knew.

He would visit his parents for comfort.

The mysterious gateway between a woman's intuition and a man's limited reality was beginning to close off. He detected disappointment coming from his parents, directed towards him. This "glow-in-the-dark" toy lost its brilliance and needed more sunlight.

Leslie went home.

His brain was racing and wouldn't allow sleep. He had both good and bad reports from knowing the feelings of others. It occurred to him that he was better off not knowing anything, unless he was told. The few that would have the courage to confront him would also gain his respect. He could work on any flaw if it bothered others.

What he couldn't accept was those that didn't like something about him and quietly despised him. They were worse than the ones that secretly admired him.

He needed another "fix"- and it awaited him at the plant.

The long week reached its last day as Friday arrived. In that time frame, Leslie changed one hundred percent as a person, from Jekyll to Hyde. His concerns were no longer about other people; he only wanted to know how they felt about him.

He started his shift with the engineering team fitting him. Today, he was to operate the renovated foundry-alone. This would be a "solo" run. If this proved worthy, the new technology would be implemented plant wide.

He breezed through the industrial site pin-pointing problems and adjusting them. He would wander towards employees that he questioned. His discovery always had mixed reviews.

He walked to the bathroom and was confronted by a woman he had never seen before. She glared at him saying, "Take that off right now and destroy it!"

He had other plans. At quitting time, the obsessed employee didn't meet with the engineers. He kept the helmet and glove attached to his body, went to his car, and drove away. The power supply would remain activated.

He had to infiltrate his parent's feelings. Leslie needed to know why they were disappointed in him. He would find out.

The son drove towards the house he grew up in and detected his parent's emotions. They were concerned about their boy, Leslie. He was an underachiever, a failure in their eyes. They wanted him to go to college and have a career. They admitted that he was a good person; however, most people are at least that. They wanted more out of their son's life, much more. They were always embarrassed when their friends' could talk about their children: They succeeded where Leslie didn't.

He drove past the house without stopping.

In despair, he sought out his best friend, Paul.

The two had survived everything together and shared secrets. Paul would be there for him. He arrived in Paul's neighborhood only to detect a devastating reading. Paul was the man Cheryl desired. The feeling was mutual, as he was getting up the nerve to ask her out. Paul was aware that she lost her love for Leslie long ago and justified this contact.

Leslie drove his car aimlessly. He was a "man without a country." There seemed to be nowhere he could go to feel loved and wanted. He was alone. The isolated man drove to his home and left moments later with a duffel bag. He took off the helmet and glove, placing them into the bag. The sensation of knowing another person's feelings would remain in Leslie's body for several more hours. He was in Hell.

Like a homing pigeon, he instinctively returned to his job. The women in the plant were still there, anticipating his arrival. They all "felt" his presence and began to search for him. They understood the unbearable pain that devoured him. Leslie was innocent; an experiment gave him this transfusion.

Night fall arrived when he was spotted. Leslie entered the plant through the back door carrying the duffel bag. He went directly to the area where scrap metal was melted down. He approached a slow moving conveyor that carried the scraps to a furnace and tossed the bag on top of the moving fragments. He then waved good-bye to the evil technology as it was carried to the intense heat, tumbling into a vat of liquid metals. He was now at peace.

Cheers could be heard as Leslie turned around. His female support group watched him defeat Goliath and gave him a standing ovation. They knew what was in the bag. A boundary separating women from men had been reinstated! Leslie was starting to feel like his old self as he smiled at the women and gave a thumbs-up.

He then noticed someone special. It was Marcie Joplin. Her cute pear-shaped body had class. Her red rosy cheeks, wavy brown hair, and blue eyes struck Leslie. The smile and stature was a perfect blend. It wouldn't be right if this heavy set woman lost any weight. Leslie was drawn to Marcie's beauty and had to go with the momentum. He walked up to her.

"Marcie, I, I, I... have some tickets for a comedy show tomorrow night," said a nervous Leslie. "I was thinking...if you are not too busy..."

Marcie took over for Leslie. She gazed at her not-so-secret crush and asked him, "Are you asking me out?"

Leslie smiled and said, "I guess that's what I'm trying to do."

"I'd love to go to the show with you!" she exclaimed. Leslie and Marcie were the only ones to receive a worthwhile benefit from the helmet experiment. They

176

gazed at one another and hugged, with Leslie kissing the top of her forehead. Oblivious to their surroundings, they turned around and left the premises- hand in hand.

# THE POLITICIAN

THE MAHOGANY CASKET shined like a new car. Inside its satin upholstery lay the body of Red Mining. He was the most flamboyant mayor the town of Rosewood ever had. Whether you loved or hated him, Red always kept his campaign promises. Still, his wake had tension over an election that was bought.

Randy Wilson was most critical about the deceased. He lost the election to Red. "I never liked him," he said quietly. "This town should only elect a home grown candidate, not a rich boy from out of state!" he said in anger.

Randy surveyed the peacefulness of his political opponent. Rosy red cheeks blended with his fine, graying red hair. His cute, smug smile remained with him even through death. As always, a loud 1970's three piece suit maintained his trademark. He would have been the perfect used car salesman. It was another moment of glory for Red, and Randy could do nothing to stop it.

The silence broke as the mayor's fanfare arrived. They approached the casket and viewed the well preserved body. A hush overcame the hall with the realization that their friend had hidden a terminal disease. Finally, a chuckle arose from one mourner, and laughter broke out. After all, this was a wake, not a funeral. The clever grin of control was displayed on Red's face as stories began to unfold.

Randy had enough. The role model paid his respects and left. He inconspicuously weaved through the gathering and found his way to the parking lot. Reaching for his car keys, a voice called out his name.

It was the town treasurer, Timothy Walls. "Randy, where are you going?" he asked.

"Home," replied Randy.

"I think it's time that we have a talk about things," said Timothy.

Randy hung his head down facing his car and pondered. "What do you want to talk about?" he asked.

"You need to understand why Red was elected," said Timothy. "It was all about *the times*. He was the only one here who could afford to do what we couldn't. That man actually respected you very much."

"Do you expect me to believe that?" responded Randy.

"Will hear me out over a cup of coffee?" Timothy asked.

Randy paused a moment in deep thought, then slapped his hand against the car. He said, "Okay!" and turned toward Timothy. The men looked at the coffee shop across the street and instinctively walked towards it.

They chose a back corner table for privacy. The situation was awkward. The election had tainted this childhood friendship. Finally, both tried to talk at the same time, which enhanced the confusion. The moment calmed when the server interrupted to take their order. Coffee would be enough for this conversation.

Eventually, Timothy spoke first. "This town loves you and wants you to run for mayor."

"I have already tried that and lost," replied Randy. "I don't want to experience that rude awakening a second time."

Timothy became frustrated and began to explain. "You were right about a rich boy from out of state getting elected. This town was bankrupt, and he talked with his money. He even promised to accept the position without pay. We could only afford him and had to gamble. You would be a great mayor now that our economy is better. This was all out of your control."

"A small town like this will never be rich and will always struggle to survive," argued Randy. "We really weren't in that bad of shape then."

A neighboring table couldn't help but overhear the conversation and made a comment. "Oh, yes we were!"

Randy and Timothy turned to the table next to them and saw Dale Walker and his wife, Marlene.

This retired couple worked with the neighborhood food bank and volunteered with many other charitable organizations.

They addressed Randy. "We are home grown like you. A town like this will never be known for its wealth. We do as much as possible for free, like Red Mining did. You are younger and need an income. As a mayor, the only way to pay that salary would be to raise taxes. Too many of us were out of work at that time. Red arrived in town with experience and money. He also wanted to be mayor and promised to do the job for free. We had no choice but to elect him. We admit that we felt guilty not voting for you based on that."

Randy sat down and let the information digest. He rolled his eyes in protest as the conversation continued.

Timothy spoke. "Randy, times *were* that hard. I would know, being the town treasurer. The local government jobs are currently filled by those who were willing to accept pay cuts. Nobody can survive on that alone. We fill those positions with retirees or families who have other sources of income. Red was free because of his wealth."

Randy rebutted with a grin. "What about the casino?"

"The casino endeavor was an act of brilliance," answered Dale. "He lured them in by showing cheap acreage for sale. He tantalized the neighboring town and tricked them to compete. He allowed them to win.

Now, they have to contend with the riff-raff. We boosted our economy with tourism. Our shops, hotels, and restaurants got busy. Most importantly, we are still the town of Rosewood."

Randy continued his argument. "Do you think that it's fair to own all the property that surrounds Pine Lake?"

Dale countered. "That is a good point," he said. "It was a strategic victory when he bought all that property!"

Randy volleyed back, "I don't understand that comment. I would have sold it to the casino and created jobs."

"No, Randy," injected Marlene Walker. "It was all about the water rights. That property was the last privately owned land before the mountain range. It held all the water rights for the communities downstream. He bought it before someone else could. This community is now subsidized annually by other counties. We would have lost this town if those rights weren't secured."

Randy absorbed the lesson. "So, he wasn't that bad after all?" he asked.

"No, he was just different," said Timothy. "The man had a unique brand of humor and liked to 'get your goat.' Red played practical jokes on occasion. He also lived alone, and we wondered if he ever had a family. We still don't know what to think of him, but he did look out for us."

Randy nodded his head with an understanding.

"There is more," said Timothy. He reached in his pocket and pulled out a letter. "This is a final request from Red. A small group of us have been invited to his house to fish. He left the keys hidden under a stone next to his mail box with further instructions."

Randy asked, "Who was invited?"

Timothy responded, "John Smith, George Thomas, you, and myself. I already talked to John and George, and they asked if we could meet at Red's place this Saturday morning."

"I'll be there at sunrise," said Randy.

Saturday arrived. Randy left his home and drove to Pine Lake. Once there, he traveled the dirt road that led to Red Mining's house. His friends were already there holding fishing poles. Randy grabbed his pole and left his car.

"Good morning, Randy!" exclaimed the anglers.

"Good morning!" responded Randy.

The overgrown lawn was a reminder of this unoccupied residence. The foursome looked at Red's retreat in silence. Timothy walked up to the mail box and saw a lone rock next to it. He rolled it over, and found the keys with a note underneath. He picked up the items and read the note to his friends.

"Gentlemen, I am grateful that you could come. If you look towards my dock, you will see my boat is ready to go!" The group looked at the edge of the lake. They saw Red's fishing boat under an awning with four life preservers inside.

Timothy continued to read. "I have a special request. I want Randy to enter my house alone and follow the black tape. Thanks, guys, and have a great day fishing! Love, Red."

The group looked at one another, not knowing what to think. Timothy handed Randy the keys. Randy placed his pole on the ground and unlocked the front door. He cautiously entered. There was another note on the main entryway floor. "Top of the day to you, Randy! Follow the tape. Your friend, Red." He proceeded.

Red Mining was an extravert in the public eye but a loner in private. Randy felt honored to be allowed access to his home. The house was beautiful! It had polished wooden floors with antique furniture. A wood stove accented the country charm along with scenic wall hangings and brass light fixtures. Tiffany lamps matched leaded glass windows as Randy toured this rustic dwelling. Like the trek to Oz, he followed his path.

He was led to a hallway that had Red's life choreographed in pictures. Many had him accompanied with smiling children. This illustrated that Red had loved ones. The tape led to a partially opened door that had a note taped to it. It read in bold print: "Please read the contents below, then enter!"

Randy could see that this was Red's bedroom. The six inch opening gave a view of his bed and nightstand. On the stand was a picture of Red Mining looking directly back with his humorous grin. It also had another note next to it, obviously meant for Randy. First, however, Randy read the note on the door:

"Randy, you made it! Come on in, the water's fine!" Randy followed Red's instructions and pushed the door as he entered the room.

Red struck for the last time. A pail of water rested between the top of the door and door jam. It turned upside down as it fell on top of Randy. The pail momentarily covered his head as its contents drenched him. He threw it off in a second, but it was too late. He looked at Red's picture and could feel his laughter as he gazed back at him. Randy was angry! He approached the night stand and read the note. It said:

"Hey, Randy, you're all wet! Don't worry though, you could be six feet under like me. There is an important reason why I asked you to be here. This town needs a mayor, and I recommended you. That's because you are by far the best choice. The township loves and respects you, just as I do. They also need you. You will make a fine mayor!" Randy began to cry with mixed emotions about Red. There was more to the note.

"There is also something special that I want to give you. Please look on the floor." Randy looked down between the small stand and the wall. He spotted an antique fishing pole. He continued to read.

"This fishing pole has been in my family for generations! My great grandfather had it and gave it to my grandfather. My father then received it as a gift and willed it to me. I now want to will this heirloom to you. It's almost one hundred years old and works like a charm! Please accept this gift and take care of it!"

Randy picked up the vintage pole, realizing that it was

185

a classic. He began to cry. There was one last paragraph to be read.

"Randy, look in the refrigerator. The kitchen is down the hallway." Randy took his new pole and left for the kitchen.

The kitchen was a show room like the rest of the house and had ceramic tile floors. A wooden counter with bar stools surrounded stainless steel appliances. The dining room was adjacent to the kitchen. A sliding glass window gave access to a deck overlooking the lake. He walked up to the refrigerator and opened it. Inside the clean refrigerator was just one item. It was a six pack of Randy's favorite beer with a note taped on it. It read:

"Attention, this beer is for none other than Randy Wilson himself! Absolutely nobody is allowed to touch this product without Randy's permission. If you do so, heavy fines will be implemented! Now go out there and catch the biggest fish of the day, Mayor Wilson! Love, Red Mining."

Randy smiled in approval and grabbed the beer. He marched out of the house with his gifts and approached his friends. He looked at them with determination and said, "Let's go fishing!"

# The Discovery of Teddy Downing

# THE DISCOVERY OF TEDDY DOWNING

THE LUNCH BELL RANG as students migrated to the cafeteria. Hastily, the hungry pupils got in line to select their tasty meals as friends united to share lunch. The laughter filled the hall as half-time arrived. Clusters of the many cliques gathered in their usual spots, with recess waiting outside. It would then be decided who would be picked for what team and what game would be played. The "in crowd" seemed to be where Steven Choy and his friends sat. They were known to be the nicest kids in school as well as the most respected. Alone in the corner sat Thor Downing, the biggest boy in school. He was intimidating and was always avoided out of fear. His large stature seemed to belong in junior high school, not elementary. He never smiled and looked mean. There was a reason why Thor never showed happiness; he didn't have any friends.

Steven Choy arrived home after school. He was an

honor student who always addressed homework first and immediately went to his room to do his assignments. He began to study, completing his homework just before dinner.

Moments later, he went downstairs as his mother started to serve supper. Family recipes from the "old country" graced the dinner table as Bernard Choy addressed his family.

"How was school today?" asked Steven's father.

"I had a good day," replied Steven. "How was your day?"

The grateful dad looked at his son and said, "Terrific!"

The parents smiled at their son as the questions were now directed at Steve's younger sister. "Anna, now tell us about your day," the father continued.

The daughter shared her day's events with her family. Like her brother, she too had a good day at school. The four enjoyed dinner as conversation continued in this warm household. Mrs. Choy had once again prepared a delicious meal, with her two children and husband giving praise to the chef. Then, an important issue was discussed.

"Steve, did you invite your friends to your birthday party?" asked Mr. Choy.

"Yes, I did!" exclaimed Steven. "They all received their invitations today at school."

"Great!" exclaimed the dad. "You probably have every kid in this neighborhood going to your party!"

"Almost," said the son.

"What do you mean?" asked the concerned elder.

"Thor Downing is mean, so I didn't invite him," said Steve.

"What makes you say that?" asked Bernard.

"He never smiles and looks mean," responded Steve. "He is always alone and sometimes stares at us."

"Do you ever talk to him or include him with your friends?" asked the probing father.

Steve thought for a while, and said, "No."

"Does he have any friends?" asked his dad.

"No," said Steve in a somber voice.

"Why don't you be the first one to do something about that?" suggested his father.

"Do you think he is actually sad instead of mean?" asked Steve.

"Wouldn't you be sad if you didn't have any friends and classmates were afraid of you?" asked the wise man.

Steven started to think with the realization that he and his friends were misunderstanding Thor. He would now look at his classmate and neighbor differently.

"What are you going to do about this?" asked his dad.

Steve thought awhile, then looked at his father with

excitement, asking, "Can we go to Thor's house tonight and invite him to my birthday party?"

Mr. Choy was proud of his son as he got out of his chair and hugged the boy. "I am so proud of you!" he said in tears. "That will make his life and yours even better!"

Steve was full of enthusiasm as he quickly made a birthday invitation for Thor. The father and son got their coats on and prepared to walk to Thor Downing's home.

"Bye, girls," said Bernard. "We should be back within an hour." He opened the door, and they left on their mission.

The duo walked down the street and turned the corner leading to Thor Downing's residence. As they approached the structure, an aura could be felt. The house seemed barricaded from the neighborhood. Overgrown grass accompanied with weeds and unkempt bushes surrounded this desolate spot in the community. White paint peeled with a few window shutters hanging on by one nail. Wicked trees that needed to be chopped down years ago reached out like claws in this dark abode. This gloomy property was outlined by a crooked white picket fence that surrendered to the elements long ago.

The father and son team were in a state of shock as they stared at the eerie dwelling. They smiled at one another knowing that they would soon be entering this "Addams Family" dwelling. The slanted gate was opened by Bernard as the two diplomats walked the long path leading to the neglected structure. What was once the final barrier before the main entrance was now a torn and rusted screen hung loosely on its bent metal frame. This cockeyed obstacle was jammed in a permanent open position. The porch was illuminated by a bare light bulb that cast a dreary haze over the spooky entrance. Bernard and Steve were now on the sagging wooden porch that had gaps from decay, and it swayed under their weight. The door had a dull varnish finish and a brass doorknob.

Steven had the comfort of his father's presence as his dad put his arm around him in support. "This isn't as bad as it looks," said his father. "This just shows you how lonely he is and what a difference you can make in his life. And remember son, he will also benefit yours."

With courage, Steve knocked on the door. There was a long pause building suspense; then, the doorknob began to turn. The door cautiously opened, and standing there was a short elderly woman wearing glasses. "May I help you?" she greeted.

Bernard spoke first by introducing himself and his son. He pointed out that Steve was a classmate of Thor's and that he had something for him. The woman introduced herself as Thor's grandmother, Emily. She then invited them into her home and left the room to get her grandson.

"This visit is much needed," said the father as they surveyed the old furniture that graced the unpainted living room.

The son looked at his father and said, "I never knew that he had nothing."

Emily returned with Thor. The grandson's face lit up with a smile when he saw that his visitor was the most popular boy in school. Steve smiled at his classmate and handed him the invitation. "I want you to come to my birthday party this Saturday," said Steve.

"Wow!" exclaimed Thor. "Can I go, Grandma?"

"Yes!" she answered. "You should have fun there!"

Thor then extended his hand to shake Steve's. The excited youth then asked if Steven wanted to play in his bedroom for a while. Steve looked at his dad with eagerness. Mr. Choy said, "We can stay here for half an hour." The boys screamed with joy as Thor led his new friend to his room. Emily offered tea to Bernard as the two sat down and visited.

"I am grateful that you brought a playmate for my grandson," said the gracious senior. "He doesn't have any friends and doesn't know his parents. My daughter always hung out with the wrong crowd and was unfit to raise her son. His father is in prison and always called him 'Thor.' We live here trying to make the most on what my social security will allow."

"We didn't know that," said Bernard Choy. "My son noticed that Thor was always quiet and wanted to introduce him to his friends."

Emily Downing cried over the thoughtfulness Bernard's son had for Thor. She then hugged the good man, thanking him for the much needed exposure that her troubled grandson needed. "He will have such a great time at the party!" she said.

Laughter could be heard from the hallway as Thor's bedroom became a playground. The adults looked at each other with a laugh, realizing that the fun sounds were a good sign. It was now close to the boys' bedtime. Bernard said, "I have enjoyed meeting you, and we look forward to having Thor at our home this Saturday." At that time, Thor and Steven entered the room catching their breath from the intense playtime they just had.

Bernard watched the boys shake hands with Steve saying, "I'll see you in school tomorrow, and have lunch with me!"

Thor looked at Steve with gratitude and said, "That will be great!"

Good-byes with smiles and hugs were exchanged as the Choys left to return home.

"How do you feel, son?" asked the father as they walked home.

"I feel guilty that Thor was always left out and that he really is a good person," said Steven. "But, I know better now."

"I am proud of you!" said the dad as he put his arm around the boy.

The following day at school, Steven acknowledged Thor with his friends present. This made the loner feel more accepted as all of Steven's friends realized that he was just like them! Lunch time continued with the same diplomacy. Steven reserved a seat right next to him for Thor Downing. The great evening the two boys shared the night before continued at school. Thor began to change; he was now making new friends and was actually smiling!

195

Saturday arrived at the Choy household with a warm breakfast being served. The happy family said grace and started to enjoy the feast. Their discussion covered organizing the much anticipated party. There was plenty to do to prepare for the festive occasion. Balloons had to be filled and hung with streamers and banners. Fold-out chairs, party hats, games, prizes, and a long table covered with a decorated tablecloth needed to be addressed. Pizza, soda pop, ice cream, and candy would accompany the birthday cake that had Steven's name on it.

It was twenty minutes before noon when the house was prepared for the event. The children were due to arrive at any moment. There was a knock at the door, and Steve anxiously opened it to greet his first guest. It was Thor. He was wearing clean clothes and was bathed with a fresh haircut. With dignity, he handed Steven a beautifully wrapped birthday gift. Steve grew excited that his new friend had arrived early. Thor entered the household as the Choy family greeted him, making the deprived boy feel welcomed.

Soon, the rest of the children arrived in groups with the house getting full. The party was underway! Steve was a gracious host as he evenly distributed his attention to everyone. Thor was enjoying himself as everyone took a closer look at this misunderstood boy and liked him! He seemed to become the center of attention and a welcomed addition to this network of friends. The present Thor gave Steven had great thought behind it. It was a walkie-talkie set the two could always play with. It was Steven's favorite present that day!

The party was a success! Everyone had a wonderful time as the birthday boy was celebrated. One by one, the guests left with their party favors and full stomachs. Thor stayed and helped the Choys clean up after the party. He was then escorted to his home by Bernard and Steven.

When they arrived at Thor's house, the boys wanted to play for a while. Tea was offered as Mr. Choy would have another visit with Emily Downing. The excitement from the party continued in Thor's room as the rambunctious boys played games.

"I want to thank you for including Thor," said the emotional grandmother. "He never stopped talking about Steven since you came to our home. I have never known him to be so happy."

"We were happy to have him; he's a good boy," said Bernard. "May I ask you a question?" he asked.

"Sure," answered Emily.

"When is Thor's birthday?" he asked.

"Next Sunday," she replied.

Bernard could only smile as he gained the vital information. "Do you mind if we throw him a surprise birthday party?" asked the compassionate man.

"He would love that!" cried out the grandmother.

"That's wonderful!" said Bernard. "I will be in touch with you and will start the planning."

The boys left Thor's room to join the adults. Handshakes with good-byes finished the parting. Bernard winked at Emily to emphasize the secrecy of their discussion.

The walk home began the planning for Thor's surprise birthday party as Mr. Choy revealed the plan to his son. "That's great, dad!" said Steven. "I know that everyone would want to give Thor the greatest birthday he's ever had! I'll tell everyone who was at my party today."

"This is good!" said his dad. "Everyone certainly likes him!"

The following Monday, Steven told his friends about Thor's birthday. Everyone wanted in on the planning. This would be a well-kept secret throughout the week.

Midway through the week, Steven talked to his father about the party plans. "Dad," he said. "My friends and I have come up with an idea for Thor's birthday, but it will cost money."

"What did you guys come up with?" asked the dad.

"The pizza parlor in town has a discount buffet on Sunday," reported the son. "All of our friends want to have his party there. The bakery is also next door, and that's where we always get our cakes."

"Hmmm," his father sighed. "If you are willing to sacrifice some of the family outings we have, that will pay for this."

"I agree to that," said the son. "Thor's worth it!"

"I have to agree with you!" said the supportive father. "I will tell Thor's grandmother that we will all meet there at noon on Sunday. We can be there early and surprise him when his grandmother brings him in!"

"Thanks, dad!" said Steven.

"Thank *you!*" replied the dad. They then hugged with mutual respect.

Bernard contacted Emily to coordinate the party as Steven called his friends. All were to meet at the pizza parlor on Sunday a half hour before Thor and his grandmother would arrive.

Sunday morning was a typical birthday for Thor. It was just him with his grandmother. She maintained the tradition of making him a breakfast and providing a present that her fixed-income could afford. The card that accompanied the gift expressed how much she loved him. He was grateful for the honor, but still— something was missing. Emily Downing went about her mundane chores while paying close attention to the time.

When the party was forty-five minutes away, she made her move. She told Thor that she could afford to take him out to lunch that day and asked if pizza sounded good. Thor was happy to leave the house and go to town. He answered, "Yes!" and went to his room to get ready. Little did he know what awaited him.

Within minutes, Thor was in the living room ready to go. His grandmother put on her coat, and they left for town. The walk was enjoyable as Thor held her hand in appreciation. They approached the pizza parlor at the designated time. Thor opened the door for his grandmother as she entered, leading him to the banquet room. She set him up by opening the last door, allowing him to enter first.

"Surprise!" roared the room in unison. "Happy birthday!"

Thor was in shock as all of his new friends were there to celebrate his birthday! He was then led by Steven to the head of the table and seated as guest of honor. There was an ovation as Thor looked in astonishment. Gifts were presented, and he was appointed first in line for the buffet. Emily sat with Mr. and Mrs. Choy as the noisy room commemorated this most-important occasion.

The grand finale was Thor being presented a birthday cake with "Happy Birthday Thor" written on its top. The amount of lit candles represented how old he was. The traditional challenge of blowing out all of the candles in a single try would allow a birthday wish.

The husky boy leaned over the cake, and with minimal effort, blew out all the candles. Cheers drew from the crowded room as a chorus of "Happy Birthday" instantly followed. Then everyone asked, "What's your birthday wish?"

Thor seemed troubled, as if he had to get something off of his chest. "I have always had a wish that nobody knows about," he said.

"Tell us!" everyone cried out.

"Okay," said the guest of honor. "I don't like being called Thor!" The room silenced as everyone looked at one another. "It sounds mean, and I don't like it." More silence continued.

Bernard Choy left the room. He returned in a few minutes after borrowing a pastry gun from the bakery next door. With his wisdom, he politely asked, "What do you want to be called?"

"By my real name," said the boy. "My name is Theodore. I like 'Ted' better than 'Thor.' But, what I really want to be called is 'Teddy Downing.' It's just one of those friendly names that nobody would be afraid of."

Bernard then walked up to the cake and, using the pastry gun, crossed out "Thor" and wrote "Teddy" above it. He then pointed at the correction and asked, "Like this?"

Teddy looked at the revised inscription and proclaimed, "That's what I want to be called!"

The room then gathered around the cake and discovered the young man's real name, and with it, his true identity. Today was actually "the first day of the rest of his life." He would start that journey as the person he truly wanted to be: Teddy Downing. His friends acknowledged this milestone and sang "Happy Birthday" to Teddy.

# THE FORGOTTEN COMMUNITY

THE WEEKEND FINALLY ARRIVED as the jubilant school bus took  students home. Laughter, conversations, and a little mischief controlled the shuttle as bus stops thinned out the chaos. Teddy Downing was about to reach his neighborhood check point, starting the two day vacation. His neighborhood friends rode the bus with him, but they seemed to be acting peculiar on this Friday afternoon. The bus ride continued with Teddy's friends talking "code." When the bus stopped by Teddy's house, the secretive friends shouted out, "We're here!" They filed out of the transit and started to walk to Teddy's house. The bewildered student asked himself, "Why are my friends acting this way, and how come they are going to my house?"

He approached his home and saw his grandmother with Benard Choy visiting in their front yard. Teddy's friends clustered around him as Mr. Choy greeted the child saying, "We have a gift for you!" The surprised boy was led to the back yard with curiosity. Benard pointed at a new addition to the property and asked, "What do you think?" It was a playhouse!

The church that the Choy family attended was expanding its building and needed to remove this shed. It looked like a tiny barn with a front and back door. It was sturdy like a house and had built-in benches with a table. It was perfect in Teddy's back yard and could be a dwelling on rainy days. It also featured insulation with an electric cord that could supply light for sleepovers. The use for this storage shed was countless. It also gave Teddy's home another selling point for the neighborhood kids!

"Thanks, Mr. Choy!" exclaimed Teddy as he hugged the gracious man. Immediately, the children ran to the tiny house and entered it. The door was closed to secure the privacy that the shelter offered. Benard laughed with the success the structure already created. Emily Downing arrived with a tray full of cookies and juice cartons. She offered Benard a snack as she thanked him once again for his thoughtfulness.

"I am happy to serve my church and help Teddy at the same time," said the good neighbor.

Emily then walked to the tiny barn and knocked on the door. It opened as she handed the tray to her grandson.

"Thanks, grandma!" said Teddy. He closed the door and shared the treats with his friends.

Benard visited with Emily for a while; then, hesitated that he had to go. He knew that the children had plans to do their homework in the new playhouse and upon finishing would leave for home. The kind man then said his good-byes and left.

One by one, each student finished their homework and packed their book bags. Soon, all were done with their schoolwork and left saying, "Good-bye" to Teddy. Eventually, he was the last child present and completed his assignments. He went into the house and asked his grandmother a question. "Can we eat dinner in my new playhouse tonight?"

"Why yes," answered the guardian. "That would be fun!" The small family of two set the table inside the playhouse for dinner. Moments later, Emily Downing catered in the meal. Teddy closed the door, as he shared his new quarters with the most special person in his life. They gazed at one another with the happiness of another triumph in the grandson's life. It was now getting late on this Friday evening. The next day was Saturday, and Teddy could spend the whole day in his new camp.

The young boy got up at sunrise and asked his grandmother if he could eat his morning cereal in the playhouse. "Yes you can," replied the guardian. "Dress up warm, and I will serve you where we had dinner last night." Teddy raced to his bedroom and changed his clothing. He then went to the small house and waited for his meal. Within a minute, the grandmother knocked on the door.

He opened the door and was handed a tray that held a bowl of cereal, a glass of milk, and a banana. The hungry grandson said, "Thanks grandma!" He took the tray and closed the door. Teddy was happy as he enjoyed breakfast in his new domain. Upon finishing, he stood up and leaned against the back door to survey the enclosed environment. Fate had arrived.

The back door was partially opened, and Teddy's weight made it swing wide open as he fell backwards out of the playhouse! The fall had him immediately slide down a wet grassy embankment that had thick ivy serving as a property line. The trail was steep enough to continue the swift ride at a high rate of speed, sliding under the ivy and thick brush. He traveled another twenty feet like a baseball player sliding in at home plate, finally reaching level ground and slowing to a stop. The dazed youth opened his eyes and looked up, seeing the shock of his life. He was completely surrounded by "old people!"

"I, I am sorry," exclaimed the frightened boy. "It was an accident."

"Are you alright?" asked a bent gray haired man.

"Look, it's a child!" cried out an elder woman.

"See if he would like some cookies with us," called out another man leaning on his walker.

Teddy looked in all directions and saw the youthful faces of senior citizens. They weren't angry; they were pleased! The muddy child realized that he was welcomed!

"What's your name?" asked a spunky lady, wearing a plaid shawl.

"Teddy Downing," replied the child.

Teddy stood up and began to shake hands with

everyone. Instantly, the community began to introduce themselves.

"I'm Hal," said a lanky man wearing glasses.

"I am Dorothy," said a woman leaning on a cane.

"My name is Ollie," said another man.

"I am Clara," said a graceful woman.

Many faces with many names extended their hands to greet Teddy.

He explained how he ended up on their property and asked, "Where am I, anyway?"

"You have just entered the "Beacon Hill Retirement Center," said another aging voice. "You are always welcomed here!"

"That's right!" said the small crowd.

Teddy looked around in amazement. The residents were friendly, the grounds were beautiful, and there was a pool with lawn chairs. He saw a beautiful wooden building that had a lobby and multicolored lights that lit up the walkways. It had a gazebo, plants, flowers, bushes, and bird baths! "Wow," exclaimed the young visitor. "You have everything here!"

"Not everything," claimed a resident.

"What's missing?" asked Teddy.

The elders looked sadly at one another knowing what

the problem was. A woman leaning on a cane said, "We don't have you!"

Teddy was puzzled and asked, "Me?"

"Yes, you," stated a hunched figure in the background. "We need you and other children just like you!"

"You will never understand until you get old like us," said a woman sitting at the nearby gazebo. "Children are the only guarantee that can make old people happy!"

The entire corps of seniors yelled, "That's right!"

Teddy looked down with this stunning realization. He began to feel good inside realizing why his grandmother was always happy. The youth thought about his friends and imagined how happy they could make this hidden retirement community. Looking up at the crowd he asked, "Can I bring my friends here?"

"We would love that!" responded a man in a wheelchair.

"Bring all of them!" cried out another woman sitting by the pool.

Teddy smiled and was given a tour. He then showed the trail that he slid down from his yard.

"I like that trail," said a ninety year old man.

"So do I," agreed another man.

"We need to fix it up a bit, so you can use it to visit us," pointed out an old woman.

"Do we want to keep this a secret?" asked Teddy.

"We have to," said a lanky man in glasses. "The managers here will close it off. The way it is now, you can sneak in after hours. It will be our secret!"

"Great idea!" said the aging group.

"I better get home now," said Teddy. "It was great meeting everyone!"

"You too," said the lanky man. "We will help clean this trail, but it must remain hidden!"

"Okay," replied Teddy. "When we have this path straightened out, I'll bring my friends!"

The boy waved good-bye as he started the treacherous climb back home.

Emily Downing spent the morning doing household chores and wasn't aware of the adventure her grandson had. "Your friends called and invited you to play softball with them at the park. They will meet there at eleven o'clock this morning." The Grandson loved to play softball and would spend the rest of the day with his friends.

Sunday morning arrived with the sunrise casting light through Teddy's bedroom window. The boy immediately dressed and went into the kitchen to ask his mother if he could, once again, eat breakfast in the playhouse. "Yes, dear," she said. "I will serve you breakfast like I did yesterday."

"Thanks grandma," said the grandson. Teddy left for the private dwelling. As he approached the shed, a note was folded neatly and taped on the  front door. He opened the message and it read:

"We were able to have my grandson build a slide that starts under the tall grass several feet from the back door of this playhouse. It leads to where we first met you. A rope was tied from the trees that outline the path, so you can use it to get back on your property. When you slide down to visit us, hold on tight- it's a fast ride! The note was written in beautiful penmanship and was signed: "From your new friends."

Teddy folded the note and placed it in his back pocket. He opened the door as his grandmother approached with a tray holding his breakfast. The elder handed the tray to the young man, as each wished one another a good morning. She returned to the house as he closed the playhouse door. The hungry child began to devour his meal. Once finished, he opened the back door and searched for the newly installed slide. He found it slightly extended from the tall ivy that he burrowed under the day before. His new friends had acquired sheet metal siding that was placed end-to-end and overlapped in the downward direction. This simple technique would allow one to slide continuously down the slick path without obstruction. He would still have to lay down flat to travel underneath the overgrown brush and ivy, but that was part of the fun!

With enthusiasm, Teddy crawled under the ivy and laid down feet first holding onto the metal sides. The excited boy held his breath and let go. Immediately, the steep angle caused the child to slide down the path, gaining speed as he traveled. The exhilarating ride was smooth as his weight caused a slight groove in the metal sheets. He was traveling like a luge in the Olympics, going for the gold! He saw the daylight as he slid under the last set of bushes and entered level ground. The soft green grass slowed down the human projectile, allowing a safe stop.

Cheers rose from the retirement home as their hero made his grand entrance. "Are you joining us for the barbeque today?" asked one senior.

"What barbeque?" asked Teddy.

"Every Sunday, we have a barbeque," stated another resident. "We are always allowed to invite friends. Why don't you and your friends be our guests today? You can even swim in our pool later."

"That's a great idea!" exclaimed a man with a cane.

"What time does it start?" asked the boy.

"Twelve noon," replied a woman in a lounge chair.

"Okay," said Teddy, "I'll go home and tell my friends. I'll be back at noon!"

The excited boy then entered the trail he arrived in. He saw rope tied four feet off the ground, connecting the trees that outlined the path. This made the ascent back home much easier!

The exhausted child arrived home asking his grandmother if he could invite friends over that day. "Why, sure you can," answered the mother figure. Teddy thanked her and began to contact his friends. He told them they would meet in the playhouse before noon and to bring a towel with their swimsuits.

His offer included lunch and was widely accepted. Eight children showed up at the playhouse bringing a swimsuit and towel. They gathered in the small house and looked at Teddy with curiosity. Two thoughts entered their mind: where is lunch, and why bring the suits and towels? The host announced, "It's now my turn to share a surprise- a big surprise!"

Teddy stood up saying, "Follow me!" He opened the back door and said, "This is going to be fun!" The group followed him as he waded through the tall grass. He found the sheet metal that marked the entrance to the steep trail. He demonstrated how to lay down on the indented slide and simply let go. He told everyone to bring their swim suits and towel and to allow one minute between each run. He let go and screamed with excitement as he disappeared under the brush.

Steven Choy got next in line. He sat in the same position Teddy did, holding onto the metal sides. The youth anxiously awaited the long minute; then, he let go with a scream. He slid under the brush and vanished.

Teddy arrived on time as the elders cheered his arrival. He got up and said, "I have my friends' right behind me!" A muffled scream could be heard traveling through the dark embankment as Steven Choy slid into the clearing. He finally slowed down to a stop as he rested on the greens of this oasis. He was dumbfounded as he looked around at the wonderment of the secluded beauty. He heard ovations that welcomed him as he saw the elated faces of this aging community. "Get out of the way!" exclaimed Teddy. "There are more right behind you!"

A confused Steven stood up and moved just as his sister Anna landed into the space he had just occupied. She was helped up by her brother as another guest could be heard traveling down the path. Soon, all were present and slowly looked around at this hidden paradise. The friendly smiles of the many seniors graced the setting as Teddy looked at his peers and said, "I'd like to introduce you to my new friends!"

The young and old began to introduce themselves as hands were shook and names were exchanged. The smell of barbeque hotdogs and hamburgers filled the air as a resident led the young neighbors to the picnic area. Lawn bowling, croquet, yard darts, horseshoes, and a pristine swimming pool would be the activities shared on this warm afternoon. This was a high-class resort, equipped with wonderful and caring people, and it was all in Teddy's own back yard! The crowd mingled at the picnic tables as accommodating seniors served Teddy and his friends. Questions, compliments, funny stories, and ideas dominated the many conversations as new friendships developed.

Hours of fun passed by quickly as "young children" played with "old children." It was becoming late afternoon, and the guests had to return to their homes. Teddy and his friends were surrounded by the residences that begged them to visit in the near future. "We promise!" vowed the young celebrities. Teddy escorted his friends to the passage that connected "Eden" to their world. They waved goodbye and, using the rope, started the expedition back to home.

Once they reached the playhouse, the group went inside and closed the door. They sat down and glared at Teddy in amazement. It was hard to believe that this humble friend was the gateway to the most fun they ever had, with the best people they ever met. The enrichment of having "old people" as friends and playmates created a different view towards senior citizens. It gave more options to grow, with a better understanding of life. Teddy was definitely that guy in school that everybody wanted to know, and he had the "coolest" friends!

## DEPRESSION THREADS

TEDDY DOWNING PATIENTLY WAITED to cross the crosswalk. He was safe as he was under the care of Eddie. Eddie was a retired military man of forty years. The gracious black man always had a smile and loved life. He dedicated his retirement to assisting local children. This playground monitor also served duty at crosswalks, using a red flag to stop traffic for safe passage. He was adopted by every kid in school. Teddy loved this charitable man. It was now Eddie's turn as a long-lost part of his life would be found.

"Thank you, Eddie!" said Teddy as cars stopped to free the intersection.

"It's my pleasure, Teddy," replied Eddie. "I would never forgive myself if you got hurt!" The caring man walked out into the street with his flag displayed.

Once Teddy reached the other sidewalk, he waved good-bye to his friend. Eddie's neck scarf whipped in the wind as he walked backwards waving to Teddy. The traffic continued with Teddy walking to the bus stop.

Teddy entered his home. He smiled as his grandmother stood waiting with a plate of cookies and a glass of milk.

"How was school?" his grandmother asked.

"Great!" replied the grandson. "I don't have any homework tonight. Can I visit my friends at the senior center?" he asked.

"I don't see why not," replied the guardian. "Be home by dinner time."

"Okay!" replied the boy.

Teddy hugged his grandmother and left the house. He raced to the backyard slide that led to the center. He got on board and whisked under the growth that barricaded the oasis. He slid into view as he rolled onto the grass.

"There he is!" pointed an old man.

"Teddy's here!" cried out another. Soon, there was a small gathering where Teddy landed.

It was getting cold outside as the evening approached. The gathering moved inside where it was warm. More friends showed up. As always, Teddy was surrounded by elder friends that cherished his company. The boy made his rounds, visiting everyone. He was saying his good-byes as he tried to remember what he wanted to say. There was something that Teddy wanted to point out, but he couldn't remember.

"That's okay, son," said an old man in a chair. "We always forget things. You'll remember in time."

Teddy laughed over the thought of being forgetful like an old person. He waved goodbye and walked the path back home.

Teddy returned home to his grandmother. It was a pleasant evening as the small family enjoyed a warm meal. He would go to bed early that night and be well prepared for school.

"Good morning, Eddie!" said Teddy as he approached the crosswalk.

"Good morning, Teddy!" replied Eddie.

Teddy was jolted by a haunting feeling. He had a recurrence of what passed through his thoughts the night before. Still, he couldn't remember what it was. He looked at the beautiful smile Eddie gave as his scarf secured warmth on that cold morning. Teddy walked to school scratching his head.

Recess would provide more clues to this mystery. Teddy chased a ball that went over the fence. Eddie was walking the grounds and retrieved the ball. When he approached the fence to hand Teddy the ball, Teddy noticed something. Eddie's neck scarf was made out of a distinct material. It was thick like wool with a yellow and brown plaid pattern.

There was something about the neck scarf that forced Teddy to ask a question.

"Eddie, can I ask you a question?" asked Teddy.

"Teddy, you can ask me anything you want," replied the man.

"You seem to wear that scarf every day, even in the summer," Teddy pointed out. "Why?"

"Well," answered Eddy with a big sigh, "these colors are much like your Scottish heritage. They represent what family you come from. During the Great Depression, fabric was given to families. Our family received this material from the government. From then on, we made clothes from it. Everyone in our family always wore this yellow and brown plaid as dresses, shawls, coats, and skirts." He then picked up an end of his neck scarf and waved it to Teddy, saying, "And that's where this came from!" Eddie laughed.

"It must be old," Teddy commented.

"It is!" said Eddie.

"Do you have to wash it a lot?" he asked.

Eddie leaned forward to Teddy and quietly said, "The secret is not to let it get dirty!"

Teddy laughed, asking another question. "Why do you always wear it?"

Eddie said, "Because of family! I might have members out there, and the family colors will identify me. I plan on wearing this in Heaven to find my mother!"

Teddy then asked Eddie a personal question. "Do you have any family?"

Eddie got choked up and replied, "I don't know."

Teddy was handed the ball, and he returned to his playmates.

School let out with Teddy walking to the crosswalk. Eddie was there guaranteeing safety for the pedestrians. The friends smiled at one another, wishing each other a good evening.

Teddy arrived home and promptly did his homework. He finished an hour before dinner time and asked if he could visit the retirement center. He was granted permission.

Teddy took the ride down the steep, polished metal and found himself where he was the day before. He was greeted by the masses and invited in for a visit. He was on a reconnaissance mission. The material Eddie wore seemed to have a common ground at the senior center. He said hello to everyone in the lobby, then continued room-to-room. Teddy was almost finished with his visit with only a few doors left to knock on.

He made an important discovery when he visited a man named Eli. As the old man opened the door, Teddy found the missing piece of the puzzle: Eli's living room window had curtains that matched Eddie's scarf!

Teddy's mouth dropped in amazement. "May I come in?" he asked.

"I would love that, Teddy!" said the elder black man. "You and your grandmother are always welcomed here!"

Teddy asked Eli about his curtains.

"Those aren't curtains," said the old man. "They are signal flares! My family was always united by those colors and that pattern. If any of them sees those curtains from the outside, they will know that this home is *their* home."

Eli broke down and cried like a child. The broken man shook with emotion, saying, "If any of them are left."

Teddy grinned with the realization that he was talking to a family member of Eddie's. He hugged Eli, saying, "I have to go home now; my grandma is waiting for me."

Eli hugged Teddy and thanked him for the visit. "Come back soon!" ordered the feeble man.

"I will," promised the boy.

Teddy left the complex and ran home. He told his grandmother all about Eddie, Eli, and the old fabric.

"You left out someone," said the grandmother.

Teddy thought for a while and asked, "Who?"

"God," she replied.

Teddy smiled and nodded his head in agreement.

"Let's invite Eddie for dinner tomorrow night," Emily suggested. "We can have dinner in the senior center cafeteria and surprise Eddie and Eli!"

"Wow!" exclaimed Teddy, "that's great!"

The next day, Emily made arrangements with the retirement home, and Teddy invited Eddie to dinner.

"You are inviting me to have dinner at your home tonight?" asked Eddie. "I'd love that!"

Eddie knew where Teddy lived from the times he assisted the school on field trips. He was told to arrive at six o'clock that evening.

The evening was set. It was several minutes before six when a knock was heard on the door. Emily answered the door and welcomed Eddie. He was dressed formally and wore his scarf. Teddy entered the room, and the three held a brief visit in the living room.

"We have a special treat tonight, Eddie," said Emily. "We are going out to eat. It's in the neighborhood, so we can walk there. This will be fun!"

"I love to walk!" said Eddie.

The three left the house and walked to the retirement home. As they approached the main entrance, Teddy and his grandmother "set-up" Eddie. They arrived at the main entrance that exposed the front of the building and Eli's curtains. Teddy stopped Eddie and asked him if he noticed anything special about the front of the building.

While he inspected the structure, Emily went to Eli's room and had him look out the window, asking him the same question. The grandmother and grandson smiled at each other as the two men looked around for anything unusual.

The motion of each one searching high and low got

the other's attention. Then, their eyes met with the family colors displayed. They were related! Eddie gave a huge smile as he waved his neck scarf to the man in the window. Eli waved at Eddie, pointing at his curtains. Eli motioned Eddie to come inside. Eddie ran to the building crying, "Oh my God, I can't believe this!"

Teddy followed as the two men met in the lobby. They cried out each other's names, saying, "I can't believe it's you!" They embraced, sobbing. Teddy and his grandmother looked in approval. They left for the cafeteria, leaving the men alone. A crowd of seniors were now witnessing the reunion. They stared down the hall at Teddy. They knew he played a role in this great moment of life.

Teddy and his grandmother sat in the dining room and visited with their many friends who lived there. Soon, Eddie and Eli arrived, wearing matching neck scarves.

"Let me explain what happened long ago," said Eddie. "My brother Eli was banned to fight in the Korean War because all of the other males from our family were already fighting the war. He ran away from home and changed his last name so that he could serve this country as a soldier."

Eli continued. "I took the name out of the phone book. The military changed all my identification to the name "Bacon." I was stuck with that last name if I wanted to get my medical benefits and social security."

Eddie said, "We never knew of the name change or Eli even being in the services. Dad died months after we enlisted, and Mom was remarried in a short time. We decided to change our last name to "Joiner" because it was her new name. We didn't want her to feel distant from any of us. For that reason, we couldn't find Eli.

Eli replied, "I couldn't find my family anymore. We now realize that we're the last survivors of our family."

"What will you two do now?" asked Emily.

"I want to work at the school with my brother!" exclaimed Eli.

"He starts Monday; I assist in hiring!" said Eddie.

The following Monday, Teddy approached Eddie's walkway. There was something different this time, however; there were two men on patrol, and they were each dressed the same. They saw Teddy and presented him with a beautifully wrapped present.

"Open it up!" said Eli.

"Yes, open it!" encouraged Eddie.

Teddy put his school books on the ground and opened the present. His eyes lit up as he looked at the brothers.

"Put it on!" they exclaimed.

Teddy reached in the box and pulled out the most wonderful neck scarf a boy could ever want. It was plaid with yellow and brown colors. He wrapped it once around his neck and looked up in pride.

"It's important that you wear this on occasion," said Eli. "That's right," said Eddie, "you're family!" The three hugged with gratitude as a family tradition stayed alive.

# VALENTINE'S DAY

TEDDY DOWNING patiently waited for the kitchen timer to detonate. The hot oven was baking cookie dough as another tray of chocolate chip cookies neared completion. Large oversized padded gloves protected the child's hands as an equally proportioned apron covered his clothing. His grandmother smiled as the boy baked cookies for the first time. This labor of love was dedicated to the local food bank. If they didn't provide the household food upon need, the family of two would go hungry. Teddy always gave thanks to that local charity by way of a homemade card. He was now getting older and wanted his grandmother to teach him how to bake cookies. This would allow him to show a much deeper appreciation to the volunteers that served them. Little did he know- that this act would grow to change the entire neighborhood.

The timer buzzed, signaling the baker to remove the

223

last sheet of hot cookies. "Be careful," cautioned his grandmother. "It's easy to forget how hot the trays get when baking."

The studious grandson carefully placed the final batch of cookies on the counter. He then smiled at his guardian and asked if he could eat one.

"Yes," exclaimed the elder. "They always taste best fresh out of the oven. Let's have milk and cookies together!"

"That sounds great grandma," said Teddy.

The grandmother set two glasses of milk on the kitchen table with matching plates. They sat down together and sampled the delicious treat.

"Mmm," Teddy sighed, "this is good!"

"Yes they are," replied the grandmother. "You will make everyone happy with these cookies!" They smiled at each other from the results that came with their teamwork.

"You have plenty of cookies for the food bank," stated the mother figure as she counted the pastries. "Why don't you also give some to your friends at the senior center?"

Teddy's face lit up with excitement! His guardian knew how much he loved visiting the retirement home.

"Wow, that would be great!" responded the child.

"Well, you might as well get ready," said the grandmother. "You are going to be very busy this morning delivering cookies and visiting with your friends."

Teddy took off the apron and hugged his grandmother as she placed the cookies in separate lunch bags. "I'll be back for lunch," cried out the boy as he donned his jacket and left with the gifts.

The first stop would be the food bank. After all, the ingredients this gift consisted of came from there. He now created a special treat out of it and would show his appreciation.

"Good morning, Teddy!" greeted the staff as he cheerfully presented the baked goods from his household.

"I made these cookies myself," proclaimed the boy. "My grandma and I want to thank everyone for giving us food when we need it."

"We are proud to help you, Teddy," replied a volunteer.

A remark could be heard that sounded like a protest. "You mean that I finally get a treat this month?" The comment came from Grace Moore, a middle-aged helper.

"What do you mean?" asked Teddy.

"This is the month where you either are remembered or you're not," replied the woman. "February can be a cruel month if you aren't loved. But, not this year! At least Teddy Downing did something." The sadden woman walked away.

Teddy didn't know what to think. He distributed the cookies as he thanked everyone for their help. It was now time for his next stop: the Beacon Hill Retirement Center.

The courier walked towards the center, bewildered on what was just said. He didn't know why this month was "different" from the others. The senior housing came into view as Teddy approached the complex. The moment he entered the lobby, he was recognized by a fanfare that gathered around him.

"Good morning, Teddy," exclaimed an old man that joyfully tapped his cane against the welcomed guest.

"Teddy!" exclaimed a woman that ran up to him and hugged him with both arms.

"Teddy's here!" announced another voice as canes, walkers, wheelchairs, and residents flowed down the hallway to see their favorite son.

"My grandma taught me how to bake cookies today, and I brought some for everybody," said the young star.

"Well good," said a faint voice. "How is your grandmother anyway?"

"She is fine and wanted to make sure that I made enough for everyone," said the caring youth.

"You tell her that we appreciate that and that we all say hello," replied a nurse.

The enthused child began to hand-out cookies to the many extended hands that surrounded him. One-by-one, a trembling hand would accept a cookie as loving eyes would gaze in admiration at this wonderful boy. Many thanks with handshakes and hugs were exchanged as the excited elders savored their treat.

Teddy stayed and visited for a half hour. He knew that his cookies were "lightning in a bottle" and would incorporate this diplomacy to make his friends happy. He even had a few left at home! Before leaving, the young man noticed a small group of women sitting together in the lobby. This site jarred the recent memory of what a woman said at the food bank. He walked up to the group and asked if he could talk about something.

"Why sure," they exclaimed.

Teddy was reluctant to address an issue that could be sensitive, but he needed to know. "Is the month of February a bad month for some people?"

The women were stunned to hear such an advanced question coming from a child! They looked at one another to confirm that he had indeed asked a sacred question. Finally, one of the ladies spoke out. "It can be the worse pain a woman could ever feel." The others nodded in approval.

Another woman said, "My sisters and I always called it the "Saint Valentine's Day Massacre."

Teddy looked at the great grandmothers in astonishment and asked, "Do you mean that Valentine's Day is a bad day?"

"No, no," corrected the oldest woman. "It is a great day that is forgotten too often."

"My grandma and I always have a good Valentine's Day," defended the boy.

"That's because you care about others," answered a feeble woman in a wheelchair. "These cookies are delicious. What made them special is that you took the time to make them for us. That's one of the many reasons why we love you so much. Most men refuse to be that thoughtful."

"Valentine's Day is the  time of year that every woman and every little girl look forward to. They dream of being honored with a valentine, just as a child wants to get a Christmas gift from Santa Clause. If they are forgotten, they feel unworthy,  unappreciated, and unloved. They are rejected. What your cookies did for us today is much like Valentine's Day; you made all of us happy. Valentine's Day, however, is the true test for any female. Some women have gone their whole lives having never received one. That's one of the worst pains a person could ever feel."

The women felt vindicated, sharing this plight. In unison they said, "Amen."

Teddy realized that the happiness he and his grandmother shared on Valentine's Day was a simple achievement. There was actually very little effort involved to commemorate the holiday. It was only a simple matter of not forgetting that special day. He now had to spread the word- to his male friends.

Teddy arrived home to his grandmother and shared the information he was told about Valentine's Day. She paused for a while looking at her grandson and said, "They are right. It can be a very painful experience to any woman that is forgotten on that day."

Teddy looked at her and asked, "Have you ever been forgotten on that day?"

The woman looked down and said, "Every year, but that all changed when I got to take care of you!" She then looked at her grandson and giving a hug said, "I love you." Teddy thought about all of the women that had never received anything on that day. It was time to take action.

The compassionate grandson called several of his neighborhood friends. He wanted to coordinate a meeting and asked if they would meet in his playhouse at twelve noon. He specified that this was a secret meeting for boys only and to bring as many as possible.

Noon time arrived with eight boys sitting inside the clubhouse.

"What's up, Teddy?" asked Steven Choy.

"You wouldn't believe what I found out today," exclaimed Teddy.

The group of boys gave their attention to Teddy. They knew that it had to be important for him to summon a secret meeting. "What is it?" asked the group.

"Okay," said Teddy. "The month of February is special to all girls, even to mothers and old ladies. It is either very happy or very sad for them."

"What do you mean?" asked Colin Wells.

Teddy sat back looking at the others. He paused briefly and said, "Valentine's Day."

The room silenced as the boys looked at one another.

Steven Choy spoke out first. "My mother hugs my dad every Valentine's Day when he gives her a valentine. Last year, my sister was hurt because she didn't get one. I guess that I should have got her one."

"That happened at my house last year," exclaimed Colin. My mom was very happy because she was remembered, but my sister and aunt cried because they weren't!"

The other boys also had stories about watching relatives cry on Valentine's Day because they were forgotten. The room was sad with the understanding that they could have prevented this pain.

"We can do something about it this year," suggested Teddy."

The boys were in tears realizing what this holiday really meant to women. "Let's do it!" they cried out.

"It's not just at home-it's the whole neighborhood," said Teddy.

"Let's do something for everyone that has been left out!" said Jeff Smith.

"Agreed!" said the boys.

Teddy served as chairman as the meeting continued.

"We need to visit the guys at the retirement home; they will be a great help," said Teddy.

The boys left the playhouse and walked to the retirement center.

Their visit would not go by undetected. As they approached the center, residents recognized the boys and spread the news of their arrival. The main lobby was immediately filled with canes, walkers, wheelchairs, and many smiles.

"What a pleasant surprise!" stated a senior.

"Teddy, you and your friends are always welcomed here," said a ninety year old woman.

"I hope that you boys will join us for lunch today," said a man leaning on a cane.

The boys visited with the residences as Teddy found a group of men playing cards.

"Can I talk to you guys about something?" asked the boy.

"Why yes, Teddy- you can talk to us about anything," stated one of the men.

Teddy explained to them about the pain Valentine's Day could cause for women. He wanted to unite with the men in the retirement center and organize a Valentine's Day that would honor every woman in the center, as well as the whole neighborhood.

"You are right," exclaimed one of the men. "It's painful for any woman to be forgotten on that day!"

"We can help you with this cause," said another man.

"We need to include everybody, but it has to be kept a secret until we have a plan," said Teddy.

"We need to have a secret meeting here tonight to plan this out right," said a senior. "Today, a local church is dropping by to give all the women manicures. We can meet in the auditorium while they are being taken care of."

"What time will this be?" asked Teddy.

"Every Sunday evening the church visits our community to donate their time for us. They always arrive here at six o'clock."

"I will gather more friends from the neighborhood and bring them to the auditorium at six," said Teddy. "Remember, it's a secret, guys only!"

"You don't have to worry about us," said one of the men. "We'll see you and your friends tonight at six in the auditorium."

Teddy smiled at the old men and returned to his friends. They continued their visit in the lobby for another twenty minutes and then left for home.

"What did they say?" asked Steven.

"We are to come back tonight at six o'clock and have a secret meeting- for guys only. We are to bring as many friends as we can," said Teddy." I will go to the food bank and let them know; get whoever you can."

"Okay, Teddy," said one of the boys. "We'll see you at

the retirement center tonight."

The band of boys split up, with each going a different direction. They were now on a mission to recruit others for the meeting. Teddy went straight to the food bank and continued his campaign.

"I have never thought about that before," exclaimed Tom Prosser. "I didn't realize that working at this food bank could have an effect on Valentine's Day. I now realize that we have been forgetting the women that we serve and the ones that we work with."

Teddy stated, "All of us never realized the pain that they went through. None of us were aware what it meant if they didn't get a valentine on that day. But we can do something about it this year!"

Teddy then told the "male portion" of the food bank about the secret meeting at the retirement center.

"Thanks, Teddy, said Tom. "I will be there tonight!"

"So will I," answered another volunteer.

"We will let the other guys know about this meeting," said Tom. "Teddy, I need to thank you for bringing this to my attention. I feel bad about this and want to help."

"Great," Teddy replied. "I'll see you tonight at six!"

The meeting was about to start at the senior center. The women were assembled in another part of the retirement center and would not detect the influx of "male visitors." The "males" quietly filled the front seats in the auditorium as six o'clock approached.

Many would walk by Teddy and tap him on the shoulder, as a support for this crusade. When it was time to start the meeting, all eyes turned to Teddy. Like a man, he walked up on the stage and addressed the audience. He gave a professional presentation about the plight women were faced with every year over Valentine's Day. He then stated that something could be done about it.

At once, everyone began to participate.

Benard Choy stood up first and said, "Teddy is right! We are overdue to make Valentine's Day a more celebrated holiday."

Tom Prosser was next. "I never knew why some women were hurt during this time of year- until Teddy explained it to me. We can accomplish a lot if we work together on this!"

An old man stood up. "My name is Hal Johnson. We can utilize our arts and crafts room to make valentines and paper flowers for all the women we know, including children."

Another man stood up and introduced himself. "My name is Milt Freeman. We often have musicians perform here on Sunday evenings. We can coordinate a Valentine's Day party right here next Sunday, on Valentine's Day!"

Benard Choy spoke out again. "My bakery can donate Valentine cookies that are heart-shaped with pink frosting!"

Teddy pointed out that he recently learned how to bake cookies and offered help to Mr. Choy.

"I am in charge of the cafeteria," said a gracious man. "My budget will allow me to cater a dinner on Valentine's Day. We will be able to provide for many!"

"I work at the food bank," injected another. "We can help supply this banquet and will be proud to assist in every way possible!"

The congregation kept rotating ideas, with everyone volunteering to help.

The room agreed on what had to be done and divided into small groups. It was soon decided on "who" would help with "what." The "when and where" was also scheduled. Soon, everyone had an assignment- with a place to perform their task. The retirement center would now send out open invitations to the food bank and community centers. Banners would also be displayed in the neighborhood to further extend the announcement. The invitations read as followed:

Valentine's Day Party
For all women, young and old!
Sunday, February 14th- Valentine's Day 6:00 PM
At
The Beacon Hill Retirement Center
Dinner, Music, Friends, and Valentines for all!

Teddy's Valentine's Day movement was now in motion. It was Sunday, the 7th of February. Valentine's Day was one week away- and there was much to do. He returned home to his grandmother and told her about the secret Valentine's Day meetings- and what he and his friends were going to do.

The grandmother hugged her grandson and said, "I am so proud of you Teddy; you always care about others! Make this the most special Valentine's Day any woman in this neighborhood ever had!" It was agreed that this week after school he would assist anyone that needed help organizing the party. He would first help Mr. Choy bake cookies.

The banners were hung down the main street of town with invitations passed out at every community service. The news traveled fast about the upcoming Valentine's Day party. Beauty salons, supermarkets, bus stops, and classrooms were all talking about this party for women, "young and old." Teddy and his friends would smile at one another every time a schoolgirl would get excited and talk about the party.

The all-male committee would have a final meeting to assign "who" would cover "what" station serving the party. The guys would show up two hours early to decorate the large cafeteria, set the many extra tables needed, and prepare the food. They were to dress formal to "look the part."

It was now Valentine's Day and getting close to four o'clock. Teddy was getting ready to leave for the retirement home. His grandmother looked at the young man and said, "I am so proud of you!" He then smiled at her and presented her a valentine he made in school. The grandmother accepted the gift as she hugged the boy.

"This is going to be great, grandma!" exclaimed Teddy. "I want you there so that I can serve you dinner!"

"I will be there," she said.

He then left for the retirement center.

The cafeteria was full of helpers when Teddy arrived. Mr. Choy brought the heart-shaped valentine cookies with pink frosting that Teddy helped bake. The elder men that worked together with Teddy's friends displayed the many valentines and paper flowers they created. A local florist got involved by providing a red rose for each woman that would attend. The local food bank was able to provide some of the food. All would seat the guests, help in the kitchen, serve, and bus the tables. The band showed up and began to set the stage they would perform on. The last minute preparations worked in harmony. The cafeteria was now ready for the evening!

The exhausted crew marveled at the festive dining hall. They felt good inside- knowing that "this" Valentine's Day would be different.

"Stations everyone," called out an elder man. The first group of women entered the hall and the party was underway! The servants went to their assigned areas as the room began to fill with the honored guest. The crew took turns opening the lobby doors for the women and escorted them to their tables. Each would be handed a red rose.

Lavish silk dresses, jewelry, and beautiful hair styles were the theme as lovely ladies arrived in droves. Six o'clock finally came, with the cafeteria almost entirely full. The band began to play classic music as dinner was served. The social brought smiles to every woman and every man.

Teddy noticed his grandmother and went to the kitchen to serve her dinner. The elated grandmother saw the small set of hands place the plate of food in front of her.

She looked at the server and smiled to see him doing a professional job as a waiter. He was handsome and wore a suit; he was a young man that day.

It seemed that every woman in the community was there. Laughter, great food, music, a rose, and valentine made this the most precious Valentine's Day- ever! After dinner, the women then got on the dance floor – and danced! They would get together and dance in groups as the fun continued. Any male that was caught standing around was immediately pulled onto the dance floor.

"Wow," exclaimed Teddy. "This is fun!" The popular boy was a marked man. He was continuously taken to the dance floor and paraded around.

The band stopped playing as the manager of the retirement home got on stage to make an announcement. "I would like to welcome everybody to the Beacon Hill Valentine Party."

The room cheered in acknowledgment.

The speaker continued, "I think everyone here knows how this occasion got started. To honor our hero, the band would like to dedicate this next number to the person that cared enough to organize this Valentine's Day gathering. That person is non-other than Teddy Downing!"

The entire room stood up and faced Teddy with an ovation. The band started to play as his grandmother approached the young man and asked, "May I have this dance?"

Teddy was overwhelmed with this honor and said,

"Sure."

The grandmother and grandson danced alone in front of the large crowd. Everyone watched the couple dance as they admired their most prized valentine, Teddy Downing.

## BROTHERLY LOVE

SUNSHINE WELCOMED the beginning of spring. Flowers covered lavish pastures with fragrances, introducing the new season. Birds sang as colorful butterflies graced fields where children played. The white blanket of winter was now restricted to mountain tops. This God created haven was ideal for a picnic! There was something missing though: a little girl named "Jody..."

Families arrived in the parking lot.

"Look, children!" pointed Pastor Mills, as he spotted a herd of deer.

"Spring is here!" exclaimed Emily Downing.

"Grandma, can we stay here all day?" asked Teddy Downing.

"I don't see why not," replied his grandmother.

Car doors and trunks opened with supplies being issued. Coolers, thermoses, jugs of water, and table cloths needed to be carried. Picnic baskets followed with juice, soda pop, and homemade pies. Teddy brought a duffel bag that carried recreational equipment. Soon, the reserved picnic site was occupied by the church group.

Benard Choy addressed the pastor as they set the table. "I loved your sermon this morning," he said.

"I appreciate that," responded Pastor Mills.

"This was a great idea having a picnic," mentioned Mrs. Choy. The mother then called out to her daughter. "Anna, I have a chore for you." She handed her daughter a glass vase and asked, "Would you pick some flowers for the table?"

"I'd love to," answered the child.

"Be sure to leave some for next week," injected the pastor.

The entire table laughed at the pastor's humor. Next week was the annual flower harvest for the spring parade. The day before the annual event, girls throughout the community would pick flowers from designated areas to decorate the town's float. More importantly, every girl that contributed got a brief ride on the float during the parade. They would rotate from block-to-block until all rode on this majestic platform. They would dress in formal gowns and equally share the title of "beauty queen." They won first place every year!

There was a pause of sadness as the moment reminded everyone of a current injustice. "I do hope that Jody Picket is on-board this year," said Mrs. Choy.

"Amen to that," responded the pastor.

Jody Picket was the victim of an over-protected brother. Luke Picket was the only male figure in this small household. His mother had several bad relationships in the past, causing the son to step-up at a young age. He watched over his mother and kept his sister on a "short leash." His job was to protect the family.

"The sheriff told me that several times they were summoned to their home. That boy even fought grown men that threatened his mother! He watches over the family like a hawk."

"Someone needs to talk to that boy," said an elder from church. "Last year, he didn't allow his sister to participate in  the flower harvest, and it broke her heart!"

Pastor Mills looked at the fellowship. He said, "We have made several attempts, but he has a barrier that won't allow anyone in."

Mr. Choy looked at Teddy and said, "If there is anyone that can do it, it's Teddy!"

"I agree," said a church deacon. "Teddy brings people together! Will you talk to Luke and let him understand that Jody belongs on that float with the others?"

Teddy was reluctant. He had several run-ins with Luke at school. Luke even punched him! Teddy didn't want any more trouble. He understood that his classmate didn't want to be close to anyone. "I'll try," he said quietly.

"Well good," said Benard. "At least that girl has a chance now!"

The festive afternoon continued as Frisbees flew, yard darts were tossed, and an occasional "clang" from a horseshoe would echo. Peaceful butterflies were caught, only to be released. Deer cautiously ate bread placed before them. Lunch was a "Thanksgiving all-in-it's-own," as the congregation held hands and said grace. The tranquility was like a scene out of "The Sound of Music."

The church picnic inaugurated the new season. The highlight would be the Flower Harvest and parade the following weekend. Teddy had six days to win-over Luke Picket.

The grandson returned home with his grandmother. They smiled at each other with the acknowledgment of another great day shared. Teddy was tired and wanted to go to bed early. He discussed the problems he had with Luke Picket and doubted if he could change his mind.

Teddy's grandmother did what she "did" best; she gave advice. "Teddy," she asked, "What do you do when you have a problem?"

The boy thought for a moment and answered, "I pray to God."

"Does it work?" asked the guardian.

243

Teddy smiled and said, "Every time!"

The grandmother said, "You know what to do, and everything will work out just fine."

She hugged Teddy, and together they said goodnight prayers. She tucked him in bed and kissed him saying, "Good night."

"Good Night, grandma," said Teddy. The grandmother turned off the lights and left the room.

Teddy prayed. He asked God to give him a friendship with Luke. He wanted Luke to trust the "right" people with his sister, mother, and himself. Most of all, he wanted Jody to join the other girls for the Spring Flower Harvest. Monday would be dedicated to diplomacy.

Teddy went to school on a mission. His first objective would be to accompany Luke at break time. He brought some homemade cookies to share as a peace offering. The nervous Teddy spotted Luke and invited himself to his table. The moment he sat down, Luke left. Lunch time had a different effect. Teddy again sat next to Luke. Luke stared at him and said, "I don't like you!"

"But I want to share some cookies with you," said Teddy. He then offered him a cookie.

"I don't want anything from you!" exclaimed Luke, and he left.

Teddy didn't know what to do.

When he arrived home after school, Teddy shared the day's frustrations with his grandmother.

"Our Lord has given you the tools and the time to accomplish what you need to do," she said. "Keep praying, and keep trying!"

Teddy accepted her advice and vowed not to give up.

The next day turned for the worst. Teddy saw Jody Picket in the hallway and said, "Hello!"

Luke saw the friendly exchange and attacked Teddy. He confronted him saying, "Stay away from my sister!" He then pushed Teddy down on the floor. Students gathered around the ruckus as a teacher hurried to the scene.

"What's going on here?" asked a concerned Mr. Kemp.

"Nothing," said Teddy. "I slipped and fell down." Teddy's testimony was enough to dismiss foul play.

Mr. Kemp asked Teddy if he was hurt.

"No, I'm fine," replied Teddy.

"I am glad to hear that," said the teacher. He helped Teddy back on his feet saying, "You need to be more careful."

Teddy received an answered prayer: Luke smiled at him with gratitude! Teddy realized that he was now inside his "barrier." He would allow Luke to make the next move.

"How was school today?" asked the grandmother as Teddy entered the home.

The grandson told his grandmother about being pushed by Luke. He then explained that Luke was glad that he didn't get him in trouble.

"That's what forgiveness does," she pointed out. "If we all learn to forgive, then our problems go away!"

Teddy looked at her as he absorbed the lesson.

"I bet you two become great friends one day," she continued.

Teddy hugged his grandmother over the thought of having a friendship with Luke. He couldn't wait for school.

It was Wednesday, with the Flower Harvest three days away. Teddy longed for Luke's presence, but it had to arrive on his terms. The lunchroom would be the most likely place for such a meeting. It happened!

The popular Teddy Downing found a small hidden corner in the cafeteria. Like his subject, he would eat alone. The natural surroundings drew Luke. The loner sat with Teddy and began to speak. "That was pretty cool how you handled Mr. Kemp. Thanks."

"You're welcome," said Teddy.

Luke left.

Teddy was relieved. Luke rarely spoke to any of his classmates, but he talked to him! He was getting progress in small portions, but would there be enough for Saturday?

Teddy shared the experience with his grandmother after school.

"Teddy, that was probably the best he could do," she said. "Keep praying, and keep trying. God is working with both of you."

Teddy had two days left to gain a trust with Luke. He would continue to try.

Thursday, Luke was distant. He seemed to use a strategy that guaranteed isolation. Teddy- like the others- couldn't get close to him. He was seldom seen outside of class. Friday yielded the same results. It would all come down to a show-down on Saturday. Jody needed to be a part of this year's festival.

Friday night had a surprise waiting for Teddy. His grandmother made arrangements to have Pastor Mills over for dinner. This would be the cavalry! If there was ever a time where Teddy needed extra spiritual help, it was now! He realized that his grandmother was "several steps" ahead of him.

The pastor was to arrive within the hour, and a wonderful dinner was already prepared. Teddy raced to his bedroom to finish his homework.

Teddy anxiously completed his assignments as a knock was heard at the front door. He opened the door to find their honored guest.

"Hello, Teddy," said Pastor Mills.

"Hello, pastor," responded Teddy. The two embraced in a hug.

Emily Downing entered the living room and greeted Pastor Mills. "We are glad that you could join us this evening," she said.

The pastor took off his coat as Emily took it. She hung the jacket in the closet and led their guest to the dinner table.

Dinner was ready. Roast beef was accompanied with salad, mash potatoes, and gravy. A homemade cherry pie would be desert.

They sat down with pastor saying grace. Then, a conversation arose.

"Your grandmother has told me the efforts you have made towards Luke Picket," said Pastor Mills. "We are all proud of you!"

Teddy sat up straight and grinned from the compliment.

The pastor continued to talk. "The teachers at school noticed that Luke seems to respect you. They say that you are the only one he will actually talk to. His sister Jody respects you as a good person; that makes Luke appreciate you."

Teddy digested the pastor's information as they ate.

Pastor Mills talked more. "Everyone wants to see Jody get involved with the Flower Harvest. We have no authority to force this. We feel that God selected you to bring her to us. Luke will only listen to you. Your grandmother tells me that this is attributed to you asking God for help. I couldn't agree with her more. Our Lord only works through us- if we reach out to him. Keep praying to God, and keep working on Luke."

"I promise!" exclaimed Teddy. He would pray for more help. He knew that he needed one more opportunity to get close to Luke and save Jody.

Saturday arrived with the Flower Harvest hours away. Luck would have it that Luke and Jody Picket lived next to the park where the Flower Harvest was held. A dirt trail led to their back yard from the very pasture the flowers were to be picked. Teddy would be there as a volunteer to assist parade marshals.

He was out of time and had to confront Luke. This was the final moments to plead his case. Teddy took a reserve flower basket and walked up the path that led to the Picket residence. As he approached, he saw the brother and sister surveying the activity below. Luke gazed at Teddy Downing with a stern look. Teddy was now standing in front of Luke and laid the empty flower basket on the ground.

The girls were gathering in the meadow below with their flower baskets. The officials were organizing what groups would pick in what area. Like an Easter egg hunt, the gold was everywhere! The ritual would start in a few minutes and last for several hours. Jody watched in anticipation as Teddy stared at her brother. Like an ambassador, Teddy began to debate.

"Can Jody join in?" asked Teddy.

"She has been out here long enough and needs to go home!" said Luke.

"This is a tradition with the community that includes all girls. Jody deserves to be here," exclaimed Teddy.

"She's my sister, and I will tell her what to do!" yelled Luke.

"You are not her dad; you are her brother," said Teddy.

249

"You are also the greatest brother anyone could ever have! I don't have a father either. All I have is my grandmother. You have your mother and a sister! When they need a man, you live up to it! I wish that I had a dad like you!"

Luke grinned at Teddy with the realization that someone actually knew his cause. He felt vindicated.

Teddy continued, "Everyone knows that you are a man. Nobody could be what you are for your mother and sister. Sometimes, a brother is needed too, especially when parents don't understand. Sometimes, they prevent their child from doing something good with other children, but a big brother would never let that happen. Jody needs her brother now!"

Luke stared at Teddy and buckled with the truth. He shook with emotions as tears ran out of his eyes. He looked at his little sister and saw a face of hope. He bent over to pick her up and began to cry. He placed her back down. With enthusiasm he asked her, "Would you like to pick flowers with the other girls?"

Innocent brown eyes lit up with excitement as she nodded her head up and down. Jody hugged her brother and thanked him. She was free! The child grabbed the basket and ran down the trail to join the harvest.

The brother watched his sister run through the meadow and join the others. He stood tall realizing that she belonged. Luke turned and smiled at Teddy. He then shook hands with his new friend.

# My Personal Life

# BONES

MY FRIEND BILL and I met after breakfast. It seems that time has changed things—including our diet. It was understood that we would no longer dine together. Still, that couldn't put a dent in this life-long friendship. This, however, was a special morning; we were going to visit Bones!

The drizzle of misty rain calmed the environment. Its tranquility greeted us as we left my dwelling for our venture. We always met at the same park bench, around the same time. The trail leading to this haven was dwarfed by tall trees on either side. Through the years, the trees leaned towards the trail and touched in the middle. This created an arbor that shielded one from the elements.

The swaying branches served as a moving prism that filtered penetrating sunlight. The foul weather had passed and the skies were clearing. Dazzling colors were created in this Godly path as we continued our pilgrimage. Our sacred meeting place would be exposed at the end of this corridor.

The trail tapered off into a clearing with our favorite bench resting on a knoll. Railroad ties were used as steps to this altar. These twelve steps would give access to our beloved friend. Bones came into view. He always had an uncanny knack for arriving first. His radiant smile gave a reassurance. Like Bill, he would always be there. We tackled the steps and continued our tradition. Finally, we were together again!

Bill had great stories as he graciously set the tempo. I always brought a good book and read what currently inspired me. Bones laughed in understanding as his good nature prevailed. The three of us marveled at how we had each developed as people. We were like everyone else. We were challenged with character flaws that spawned vices...but that was long ago.

The best things in life are certainly free. All I ever wanted was to stay on my path and to be close to my loved ones. Bill and Bones couldn't have agreed more. We took time to appreciate God's creation. Our panoramic view gave us majestic mountain tops, meadows, and valleys. Trees, flowers, and rich green grass with butterflies accompanied the fresh breeze of life. This was Heaven. Prayer was always in order as we bowed our heads for a moment of silence.

The visit was now coming to an end. It was time to return to my obligations. We said our good-byes and dissipated back into our daily routines. Bill and I walked down the path we arrived on. We eventually parted as he went his direction, and I went mine.

My morning was beautiful! The day would continue with visiting friends and family. My next stop would be a surprise visit at my nephew's workplace. He has a lawn maintenance business and works throughout the community. I knew his schedule and could drop by to visit anytime. That day, he was working in my neighborhood.

Steam was rising off of the moist sidewalks. A symbolic rainbow arched across the sky giving the sign for safe passage.

A bright orange utility truck that displayed "Kevin's Yard Service" was parked alongside a rustic stone wall. His crew was working meticulously. Pride showed as they manicured healthy green grass that surrounded plants, statues, bird baths, and monuments. Kevin drove the riding lawn mower with the concentration of a professional golfer. As he turned sharp to keep the grounds uniformed, he noticed me. His signature smile did his company uniform justice. A polite wave with one hand was all he could spare. I waved back with the understanding that he was busy. There was plenty of work to do that was delayed by the morning rain.

I still felt welcomed and entered through the opened gates. The crew smiled at me as they continued to work. This inner city oasis gave a peace to the community. A basket of beautiful orchids hung from a nearby gazebo. Nobody was watching. I delicately removed an orchid by the roots and quietly walked away with it.

I wanted to transplant it in a place that was dear to me. Within a minute, I dug a small hole in the fertile ground with my oversized hands. I planted the orchid as if it were always there. I stepped back and viewed the granite slab that I stood before. The inscription on it read: "Robert Joseph 'Bones' Hansen". Below the solitary name listed the date of birth and the last day of life.

The flower was an updated token of his memory. It was simple and beautiful all by itself, like the marker and Bones himself.

This day was not over. There would be a meeting tonight to celebrate anniversaries. I would once again meet up with Bill and all of his friends.

# THE SACRED BICYCLE

MOST NEIGHBORHOODS have that obnoxious rich family up the street; our neighborhood was no different.

This family had a dad that did well with his own business. In turn, their children had the best toys on the block. They went a step further and flaunted their treasures. Like monkeys on a tree, their youngest boy advanced a limb when he got a new bicycle. It had all the bells and whistles. He loved to tantalize others by asking them if they wanted to ride it. This spoiled brat would say, "No" if others answered, "Yes."

This boy would ride his bike in front of our house to get attention and showboat all the way back home. The lower income families on our side of the tracks would watch this display.

On this particular day, many of us children were playing on their end of the neighborhood. The rich boy had his prized possession parked on the sidewalk, blocking the entrance to his  garage. He was pacing back and forth as the rest of us stood abreast forming a straight line. It was like a military movie where the platoon was being addressed by a drill sergeant.

He would point at each of us specifically and ask, "Do you want to ride my bike?"

Each "friend" would answer, "Yes!" This was in hopes that eventually one of us would be rewarded for our patience and loyalty. He would respond, "Well, you don't get to," and laugh.

Then it happened. His equally inconsiderate sister left their house, digging in her purse for her  car keys. The family station wagon was parked in the driveway. It's obvious what happened.

The amazing part was that the victim's back was turned to his sister, allowing us to see a poetic justice materialize. It would only take one child to draw attention to the disaster that was about to happen and thwart it. The regiment held in tight formation and allowed the play to develop. It did.

Each sibling was too arrogant to worry about their surroundings. No sooner did the older sister open the car door than she was inside. She put the key in the ignition and started the engine. In one continuous motion, she released the emergency brake, shifted in reverse, and piloted the heavy vehicle backwards.

The mechanical noise interrupted the younger brother's thought process. He turned around to see the family car in motion. It was too late to stop the destruction of his bicycle. The rear end of this vehicle violently bounced up and down as it rolled over the bike. The process was repeated when the sister changed direction to see what it was.

She got out of the car yelling at him for making her late for an engagement. He held his ground by pointing out that she should watch where she is going. We, the audience, laughed and wanted more entertainment. It came!

The spoiled child righted his flattened bicycle and inspected it. His facial expression was that of a child forced to eat his vegetables. Like Wile E. Coyote, he verified the damage by attempting to ride it. It rode true for a quarter pedal; then it quivered violently with squeaks and groans caused by restricted movements. He would have to extend his body opposite of the listing bicycle to maintain balance. This would have been a perfect prop for any circus. We all laughed and thanked one another for allowing this to happen!

I still have nights where I laugh myself to sleep thinking about it.'

**THE END**

# EPILOGUE

I want to thank you for reading my stories. They were meant to amuse and have you scratch your head a bit. My goal was to give you a warm feeling when it's all said and done. I consider myself like a photographer who captures the unsung hero. I use a pen instead of a camera. I will write stories for the rest of my life, with the hopes that I can bring pleasure and inspire others.

Matt Shea